THE PROPER PROCEDURE
and other stories

THE PROPER PROCEDURE

and other stories

THEODORE DALRYMPLE

Published by New English Review Press
a subsidiary of World Encounter Institute
PO Box 158397
Nashville, Tennessee 37215
&
27 Old Gloucester Street
London, England, WC1N 3AX

Cover Art and Design by Kendra Mallock

ISBN: 978-1-943003-10-5

First Edition

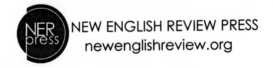

NEW ENGLISH REVIEW PRESS
newenglishreview.org

To the memory of
Dr Alan James Gardner (1936 - 1987)

Contents

- 1 -

BILDUNGSROMAN

A ND SHE HAD LEFT her native country – the land of poets and thinkers – for this!

Life in Percy Bysshe Shelley House, a concrete tower opposite its identical twin, Harold Laski House, was growing more and more intolerable. It had always been lonely there, of course, stuck up on the fourteenth floor, knowing no one, the traffic swirling far below, oblivious; but the city was so expensive that she could afford nothing better than a council flat, though she had always worked and had never had a day off sick, not in the thirty-five years since her arrival in England just after the end of the war. Not like the natives.

Always unattractive, Percy Bysshe Shelley House was now hell on earth. Miss Falkenhagen doubted whether any of its residents other than she even knew who Percy Bysshe Shelley was. What a country! The people couldn't even speak or spell their own language properly, and hardly knew that any other languages existed. They knew nothing of their own literature and cared even less; their pleasures were coarse and brutish, their food revolting, their manners, if such you could call them, appalling. It was not so much that they lacked refinement, these people; rather they hated refinement and persecuted it wherever they found or even suspected it.

Miss Falkenhagen spoke better English than they and took

9

pride, in her capacity as secretary, in never making a spelling mistake – unlike her native-born colleagues, who felt neither pride nor shame in their work. It was for that reason that she couldn't bring herself to befriend them, for what profit would there have been in doing so? Quite apart from the mental slovenliness that their lack of pride indicated, what did they talk about other than what was on the television the night before, their convoluted personal lives and their clothes? Thin mental gruel indeed for someone as intelligent as she; and it was absolutely typical of them that, though obsessed by clothes, they should be so badly dressed.

But even they were not as bad as the residents of Percy Bysshe Shelley House, for they were merely empty-headed rather than malicious. To what, other than malice, could one attribute the male residents' propensity to urinate in the common parts and in the lifts of the building, impregnating the edifice with an irremovable ammoniacal smell? They were not old men with prostate disease who could hardly be blamed for losing control of their bladders, but on the contrary strapping young men in the peak of condition. Surely even when drunk (as, of course, they often were, as often as they had the opportunity) they could have waited another minute or two to relieve themselves? No, they did it from sheer hatred of their fellow-residents, or perhaps, like dogs, to signal their control of the territory. How pathetic!

But worse than the smell was the noise. This wasn't just a question of slamming doors and the odd quarrel, the sound of which was transmitted into her flat by the thinness of the internal walls: partitions would be a better words for them really (Miss Falkenhagen took pleasure in fine verbal distinctions, especially in her adopted language). She could have tolerated that. No, it was the music, or rather the so-called music, that they played, night and day. One must not exaggerate, she thought, especially because of where she came from; but the fact is that the deep base rhythm that caused the whole building to vibrate, and the wild vocalisings that these barbarians called singing, reminded her of the inescapability of poisoned gas. Even Bach and Mozart would not have been welcome at high volume at two, three or four in the morning: but this, this eternal cater-wauling, this sub-dionysian frenzy of savages, was insufferable. She had tried, without success, to do something about it.

Of course, one could not approach the barbarians directly. At best they would laugh in your face, at worst attack you or wreak revenge on you; it was certainly no good appealing to their better nature, for they had none to appeal to. They did not understand, or did not care, that some people had to work in the day and therefore needed to sleep at night; they were nocturnal creatures, sleeping by day and occupying themselves with their loud uncouth amusements by night. How they could afford to live like this was a mystery to Miss Falkenhagen; she supposed it must be a combination of social security and drug-dealing. Certainly one noticed needles abandoned in the stairwell when one was obliged to walk up the stairs while the lifts were re-stored after a particularly destructive bout of vandalism.

Miss Falkenhagen had tried the police but, short of murder, they were uninterested in what went on in Percy Bysshe Shel-ley House. There had indeed once been a murder there, in the course of a dispute between two young men over which brand of tracksuit was best; in the circumstances you could hardly blame the police for having come to the conclusion that there was little, except for the matter of timing, to distinguish a crim-inal from his victim. It was silly, therefore, to expect the police to exert themselves over so trivial a problem as that of continu-al loud music. As the police telephonist told Miss Falkenhagen when she called, it was a matter of manners, not law. Somewhat inconsistently, she also suggested that Miss Falkenhagen try the Housing Department, that is to say her landlord.

She had done so. After considerable hesitation and with much reluctance, the Department agreed to measure the noise by means of a recording device affixed for twenty-four hours to one of the walls of Miss Falkenhagen's flat. For some reason, the device had recorded nothing, as if Percy Bysshe Shelley were a Trappist monastery. Miss Falkenhagen protested against this evident absurdity, and demanded that the device be deployed again; but she was told that resources were limited, complaints were many, and the device was needed elsewhere. Only one bite of the cherry was allowed, she was told; besides (this by way of consolation), there was little anyone could have done about it even if the device had recorded the most terrific racket. After all, even the noisy had to live somewhere.

England hadn't been like then when she arrived, thought Miss Falkenhagen. She had come because her own country, the land of poets and thinkers, had been so thoroughly bombed-out that it seemed impossible that life there could ever consist of anything other than sifting among the rubble in search of useful oddments and meals of potato peelings. Life in the victor, England, was no doubt much less comfortable than it had been before the war, but it was positively a life of luxury by comparison. She seized the opportunity to move, therefore, when it presented itself, even if it meant (as it had) that she would never see her parents again.

She saw now that it was a terrible mistake that she had made, and that she should have stayed where she was born and brought up. In the intervening years, the position of the two countries had reversed; what had been the promised land had become the cursed land, and vice versa. Poverty had become prosperity, and prosperity poverty. When she peered out of her window, she saw a city-scape that looked as if it had undergone bombardment by a new kind of weapon, one that spread concrete, brown-greyness and ugliness everywhere. It was inhuman, inhuman! You couldn't really blame anyone for behaving like a predatory beast in it.

Miss Falkenhagen began to brood. It was too late now in life to change anything very much: how insouciant one was in youth, believing any mistake or error to be retrievable because of the infinite stretch of time before one! No; in the words of that cliché (but clichés were what they were because they were true), she had made her bed and now she would have to lie on it.

She began to suffer stomach pains. She had always been healthy before, ascribing the illnesses of others to the filthy diet they ate and to their bad habits. She herself had needed no encouragement to eat healthily, for it had never occurred to her to do otherwise. It was not only inconvenient and alarming that she should be attacked by stomach pains, therefore, it was unjust.

She was reluctant to consult her doctor because she did not trust him. She had nothing personal against him, indeed she hardly knew him; it was just that she found it difficult to believe that the doctors produced by so crude and debased a country could be up to the scientific, intellectual and ethical level that real medical practice required. However, she had little choice in the matter. She had nowhere else to turn.

The doctor listened to her without evincing much interest. You might have supposed from his attitude that she was a chronic complainer, or the kind who regarded a visit to the doctor as the highlight of her week. He didn't even examine her; he simply took a pad and wrote a prescription on it. 'Take these,' he said, 'twice a day before meals.'

It was hardly surprising that she got no better. The pills did nothing except give her eructations that savoured slightly of peppermint. It was as she thought: like everything else in this country, the doctor was of low quality, sloppy and careless. But, having once consulted him, she was not prepared to let him off the hook. She returned to him several times in search of a diagnosis, if not of a cure.

Eventually he took her blood and even examined her, though only because of the reproachful intonation of her questions and her reminder that she was of an age when serious things began to happen to people. His examination was not thorough, and he touched her as if she were distasteful to him, as rotting meat might have been. It was obvious that he couldn't get it all over with quickly enough.

When she had put her clothes back on, he looked, or squinted, at her through narrowed eyes.

'Do sleep at night?' he asked.

Miss Falkenhagen described the throb of the music, so-called, through the fabric of the building, and how it rendered her sleep fitful.

'And can you concentrate?'

It was an odd thing to ask, but Miss Falkenhagen had to admit that of late she found it difficult to do so. When she settled down to a book, for example, scenes of her early life kept appearing in her mind, and she forgot what she had just read. Things didn't stick, which was most unpleasant for someone of her serious nature. No doubt some people, who had nothing much in their minds anyway, did not mind being unable to concentrate; but for her, now she came to think of it, it was a kind of torture.

'I'd like you to see a colleague of mine,' said the doctor. 'A specialist.'

'What kind of specialist?' asked Miss Falkenhagen.

'I think you're depressed,' said the doctor hastily. 'A psychiatrist.'

'A psychiatrist!' said Miss Falkenhagen. 'What has he to do with pain in the stomach?'

The doctor was uncomfortable, as if suffering from a guilty conscience.

'Well,' he said, 'the fact is that the mind is indistinguishable from the body – and vice versa, of course.'

Miss Falkenhagen remained silent.

'The mind can affect the body,' he resumed. 'Let me give you an example. If you suddenly saw a cobra by your feet you might lose control of your bowels. Your fear is a purely psychological state, but the effect on your bowels is physical. Of course, this is a very crude example but it illustrates what I mean. Mind and body are inseparable, and their interactions can be very subtle.'

Miss Falkenhagen shifted a little on her chair, but at least she did not interrupt.

'These days,' continued the doctor, 'there is no prejudice against mental illness. It is just the same as physical illness. No one would blame you for having ulcerative colitis, say, and no one blames you for being depressed.'

Well, thought Miss Falkenhagen on her way home, as the English say, 'In for a penny, in for a pound' – not that the pound was worth much these days, but then neither was the consultation with the psychiatrist likely to be.

About two weeks later Miss Falkenhagen received through the post an appointment to attend the Mary Lamb Mental Wellness Clinic. On the day appointed she slipped on her winter coat and left Percy Bysshe Shelley House in an almost furtive way, as if anyone could have told where she was going just by looking at her.

The Mary Lamb Mental Wellness Clinic turned out to be a low, rectangular brick building, obviously intended as temporary but long since having become permanent, in the grounds of the Leafields Psychiatric Hospital (formerly County Asylum). These grounds had once been extensive, but were being whittled away by financial necessity: which, perhaps, was just as well, since one of its residents a few years previously had used access to laurel bushes to distil a liquid containing cyanide, which he then administered to his fellow-sufferers.

Miss Falkenhagen entered through a metal framed door with windows in whose glass there was a wire mesh. The receptionist at the counter nearby was embroiled with a man of about sixty in an ancient pullover and very stained trousers whose cut bore little relation to his waist, buttocks or legs, and which were kept in place by several belts composed of string.

'Now, Cyril,' said the receptionist with a mixture of compassion and exasperation, 'you know that you're not supposed to be here, it's out of bounds. Go back to the ward.'

'Got a fag?' said the man called Cyril.

'Only if you go back to the ward.'

'Giss a gag, giss a fag,' said Cyril, holding out his hand.

'All right then,' said the receptionist. 'But then you must go back to the ward.'

Cyril grabbed the proffered cigarette like a hungry beast and then turned to go out, brushing past Miss Falkenhagen, who shuddered, partly sincerely and partly to demonstrate as clearly as possible that she was not like that.

The receptionist asked her to wait: Dr Brown would be with her in a moment.

Miss Falkenhagen had hardly had time to flick through the old magazines in the waiting room, and wonder how people could be content to fill their minds with such trash, when Dr Brown called her into his room. She was so surprised by his appearance that she took nothing else in about the room.

She had been expecting a middle-aged man at least, someone on the verge of retirement and at the acme of his wisdom: perhaps even a pipe-smoker. Instead, Dr Brown was a very young man, handsome, well-dressed without ostentatious attention to his appearance, slightly above average height and with a manner that, while confident enough, was not over-confident.

'I was expecting someone older,' said Miss Falkenhagen.

'I am Dr FitzGerald's assistant,' said Dr Brown. 'I discuss each case with him.'

His frank and open acknowledgement that he was not the chief reinforced Miss Falkenhagen's favourable impression of him. Only someone who was sure of his own worth, in a healthily unobtrusive way, could admit without difficulty that he was not the most experienced or important man round here, the one who decided everything. Miss Falkenhagen decided that she would get on with him.

Dr Brown was not excessively interested in the details of Miss Falkenhagen's abdominal discomforts. He assumed that serious pathology had already been excluded. And, indeed, his conversation with her seemed hardly medical at all, which again spoke much in his favour, for it indicated that he considered Miss Falkenhagen a perfectly intelligent and sensible person – which, of course, she was. It almost felt as if she were talking to a friend rather than a doctor. He didn't interrupt her, except for minor points of clarification, and altogether showed himself as a cultivated man of the kind Miss Falkenhagen always wanted to meet but (living where she did) met so rarely. You could see on his face that he was interested in her not as a case but as a person; and it was true that her life history was really out of the ordinary. You wouldn't think it from her current restricted way of life, but she had been witness to great events: for example, did Dr Brown know that she had once seen Hitler in person? Indeed, she was the member of the Bund Deutscher Mädel chosen to present him with the bouquet of flowers in front of the excited crowd that lined the street to greet his historic visit to their town. On the day, however, she had gone down with tonsillitis, and therefore someone else – a girl called Elfriede – had to supply her place. The residents of Percy Bysshe Shelley Tower knew nothing of her past, said Miss Falkenhagen, and were so wrapped up in their own sordid and petty day to day affairs that they would not even be interested in it. But what stories she could have told them, had they been interested! She was, after all, a witness to the most important years of our era. The fact that she had not been important, just an ordinary child growing up as if those years were perfectly normal (for a child, having no standard of comparison) accepts what goes on around him as being in the nature of things, eternal, unchanging and unchangeable, added rather than detracted from the interest of her memories – in her opinion, though of course she understood that Dr Brown might think otherwise.

'No, no,' protested Dr Brown. 'I think you're quite right.'

'There were other Nazi bigwigs who came to our town,' said Miss Falkenhagen, glad at long last to have met someone educated, intelligent and imaginative enough to take an interest in what she had to tell.

'You should write it down,' said Dr Brown.

His words acted almost as an electric shock on Miss Falkenhagen, for they coincided exactly with her deepest inclination. She had long thought that her memoirs would be of surpassing interest and historical importance, for the time would come, quite soon in fact, when there would be no one left to record the kind of memories that she had. Moreover, having read as much as she had, she was sure she would be able to write them down with literary grace and elegance – and in a language not her own!

'I always think it's a tragedy when someone's memories die with them,' said Dr Brown, 'especially when they concern events or times of historical importance. Once they are lost, they are lost for ever.'

Miss Falkenhagen smiled. How pleasant it was to meet a young man mature enough to understand the importance of the past. Most young people, especially these days, couldn't care less about it: for them, the present moment and its so-called pleasures were all-important. No, all-important was not quite the word, for it implied an awareness, albeit subliminal, of something other than the present moment. In fact, young people these days didn't even know there had been a past: the world began with them, and each moment was unconnected with any other. Dr Brown, thank God, was not like that.

'Writing your memoirs will do you more good than anything I can give you,' he said. 'Medicine will only give you side-effects.'

Miss Falkenhagen was buoyed by what Dr Brown said. She felt better already. It was true that what she had lacked hitherto was purpose, and this had depressed her; when Dr Brown went further, and said it was practically her duty to the world to record her memories and experiences, she was almost elated.

Miss Falkenhagen was a modest person, but there was no point in disguising from herself - for modesty did not compel dishonesty - that God had granted her an unusual degree of literary ability (for had she not mastered a foreign language so thoroughly that she made fewer grammatical mistakes in it than most native speakers, her accent notwithstanding?), and chance had put her in the way of experiences of the greatest significance, a happy combination of circumstances. The doctor, though young, was quite right: it was her duty to write her memoirs.

'As a matter of fact,' said Miss Falkenhagen, 'I had thought of writing them. They might be of some value to historians and even of some interest to the public, though of course the public is generally more interested in footballers and pop stars.'

Dr Brown assured her that, though this was true overall, yet there was still a sufficient audience for works of history: you had only to go to a bookshop to see that.

Miss Falkenhagen, who had arrived at the Mary Lamb Mental Wellness Centre in a state of hostile scepticism, left with almost a spring in her step. Indeed, she was so invigorated by her encounter with Dr Brown that she decided not to take the first bus that came along, but rather to walk a few bus-stops in the direction of home. There is nothing like a brisk walk to re-inforce a happy resolution, and Miss Falkenhagen, who in any case had never let herself go physically to seed, strode along like someone much younger than herself.

Of course, fame would not be the object of her writing, much less money – the latter was so vulgar a consideration that she quite consciously put it out of her mind, and would not let it re-enter. Had money been of any interest to her, she would not have remained a mere secretary all these years. No, her book would have a *succès d'estime*, a classic: not a great classic, like Goethe's *Faust*, there was no point in being unrealistic, but a minor one, a kind of miniature on what was nevertheless a great subject. People would continue to read it as long as they were interested in the Third Reich, which was likely to be for a very long time. Had she not heard a publisher say recently on a book programme on the radio that a swastika on the cover of a book automatically increased sales by at least thirty per cent? No doubt most of the interest of which this was indicative was morbid or prurient, but it did at least mean that there must be a number of serious persons to whom she could address herself, who were interested in the lessons of the period. The main thing was to ensure that nothing like it ever happened again, and Miss Falkenhagen's book would be a well-sculpted and enjoyable, but serious, contribution to this laudable end. Form and content would be happily united in her book.

What would she call it? She was so absorbed in her thoughts as she walked along that she hardly noticed what was going on around her, and once she almost ran over a young woman who was dragging her child along the pavement like a sack of pota-toes.

'Watch where you're fucking going, can't you?' said the coarse young woman who claimed the exclusive right to abuse her child, totally unaware that she was speaking to a person of some standing in the intellectual world.

Miss Falkenhagen was momentarily shaken, the shrillness of the woman's voice obtruding on her reverie, but quickly returned to the question of the title once the confrontation was over. What should it be, the title? Nothing catching in a vulgar way – no pun, for example, no matter how clever – yet arresting and, of course, informative. The obvious illustration for the cover would be of a blond little girl presenting flowers to Hitler, although some might say, of course, that it was not only hackneyed but misleading, because Miss Falkenhagen had never actually met Hitler. The publisher would probably insist upon it, however, and Miss Falkenhagen would raise no deep objection. If people judged books by their covers, that was their affair. And, after all, the book would be about Nazi Germany, even if the author extended her account to the immediate post-war years in England; such a cover, therefore, would not be so very misleading.

Arriving back at Percy Bysshe Shelley House, a nasty altercation was taking place in the lobby between a Rastafarian and a thin young white woman who, despite the draughtiness (a cold wind whistled through a broken window), was scantily dressed. One could easily imagine the altercation ending in violence and even murder, but Miss Falkenhagen knew better than to intervene in what did not concern her, and went straight to her flat.

Miss Falkenhagen settled to the pleasant task of thinking about her book. She was aware that she ought not to conceive of it as already written, but it is only human to daydream a little; in her mind's eye, she read the reviews and even saw extracts from them on the back cover of paperback edition. She smiled; how surprised they would be at work, all those who found her uninteresting just because she was not interested in what they were interested in. As for her fellow-residents in Percy Bysshe Shelley House, they were so utterly beyond the reach of cultivation that the fact that she had written a book would mean nothing to them. She would move out, into more congenial surroundings.

The first thing to do, of course, was to put her memories and recollections in order. No, that was not the first thing to do; first she must have notebooks in which to write down the things as she remembered them. Or would a system of index cards be better? Notebooks, perhaps, would be preferable if she were going to stick to a strict chronological account, but it might be more interesting to write thematically, with flashbacks and other such literary devices. In any case, she had neither notebooks nor filing cards in the flat, so she would have to go out again and buy some. And this would take time, because she would have to go quite far: materials for writing books were not exactly items of first necessity for the local residents. Industrial cider of high alcohol content was more in their line.

So Miss Falkenhagen went out again. She had to go to a shopping street half an hour away (if you counted the time waiting for a bus); and of course the return journey was just as long and arduous. Moreover, the first notebooks that she found did not please her. They had cheap glossy covers, with vulgar, childish pictures on them. One could hardly record scenes from the Nazi era on pages protected by pink rabbits and blue bears. One had only to look at these pictures to have one's concentration destroyed. Somehow they made you despair of the human race. How could anyone find them attractive?

It proved surprisingly difficult to find three notebooks of suitably sober design. It was easy enough to find index cards, but the plastic boxes in which they came were of horrible garish primary colours. By the time Miss Falkenhagen had all that she wanted she was tired out. The fact is that she wasn't young any more; and though thinking and writing were sedentary work, still they required energy, with which she was less plentifully supplied than in former years.

Still, she had made a start, and a good start too! One had, after all, to start somewhere: you couldn't build a house without bricks. Miss Falkenhagen went to bed happy, full of purpose; even the deep base throb of the music, whose vibration usually caused an unpleasant sensation in the lower part of her abdomen, and which started at eleven o'clock at night almost as reliably as the sun went down, did not disturb her.

On returning home from work on the following days, Miss Falkenhagen would take out her notebooks and sit at the all-purpose table in her living room and write a few notes. It was really very surprising what you could remember when you tried, even about things to which you had given no thought for decades. For example, her father had been a station-master, and she recalled not only the layout of his office, but the colour-scheme of the waiting rooms in his station (much more tasteful than anything today, incidentally). As she remembered, she wrote things down, in a mixture of German and English that only someone who was bilingual could have deciphered.

After a few days, however, it occurred to her that she might approach things differently. Most of her reading, extensive as it was, had been in literature, above all in classical fiction. She had read very few memoirs, if any; and it was surely no disgrace to admit that she could learn something from how others had approached the genre. It was hardly reasonable to expect her to produce a memoir without any knowledge of memoirs as such. All literature, after all, grew out of, and added to, a tradition. So Miss Falkenhagen went to the local library to see what she could find. It shouldn't have surprised her, probably, that in the section marked 'Biography,' to which the librarian had directed her, there was nothing to be found but the life stories of actors and actresses, sportsmen, popular entertainers and a notorious criminal or two. This was not what she needed or wanted; she decided that it would probably be worth her while to procure for herself some memoirs of more serious, if less famous people, because then she would be able to refer to them whenever she wished. Accordingly, she went to several bookshops which, of course, were not in her area. She bought the memoirs of politicians, ex-colonial administrators, journalists and more serious writers. It was best, she thought, to be thorough, and she began systematically to read through them, not starting a new one until she had finished the old, though she was often tempted to do so and some of them were very long – longer than they needed to be, in her opinion, a lesson that she would certainly take to heart when she began to write.

She had an appointment to see Dr Brown two weeks after the first, and she found herself looking forward to it as if it were some kind of treat or social event. It couldn't be, she told herself, that she was falling for him in any romantic sense or fashion, not at her advanced age and with the difference in years between them. Preposterous! She was far too sensible, if not in the strictest sense experienced, for that kind of caper. No, it was simply that someone like herself longed for a little intelligent and intellectual conversation, to talk to a person (man or woman, it hardly mattered which) for whom the petty day to day flux of existence, and the circuses provided for the distraction of the unreflective masses, were not the sole preoccupations.

Dr Brown asked her how she was.

Miss Falkenhagen did not say that she was better, because to have done so would have implied there had been something wrong in the first place. And if there was one thing that was perfectly clear, it was that her mind had always been perfectly clear: all she had needed was a little encouragement to do what had always wanted to do in any case and (if truth be told) had always been her deepest, if sometimes unacknowledged, ambition.

'I'm getting on very well,' she said.

'I'm glad to hear it,' said Dr Brown. 'And the book? Have you started?'

Dr Brown's manner was enthusiastic and eager, as if he were more of an editor than a doctor.

'Yes,' said Miss Falkenhagen, not without a slight twinge of conscience. 'I'm gathering my materials.'

'I thought it would all be in your head,' said Dr Brown.

'Well, of course it is,' replied Miss Falkenhagen. 'All the same, there are one or two books I need, and documents. I want to be as accurate as possible.'

'Well, of course, I quite agree.'

'The last thing I want is for reviewers to say, no, it was not on the thirtieth of January, it was on the thirty-first, therefore the writer is unreliable or not telling the truth.'

'Pedants can always be found to nit-pick,' said Dr Brown agreeably. 'There are books in which many facts are wrong and yet overall convey the truth of their subject. And, of course, the opposite: books in which every fact is right, and yet miss the point completely.'

Miss Falkenhagen and Dr Brown had a very pleasant discussion about the nature of literary truth, the upshot of which was that Miss Falkenhagen should return to the Mary Lamb Mental Wellness Centre in a month's time.

How well-informed Dr Brown seemed on literary matters! A real pleasure to talk to him! One might even say that he was something of a soul-mate: though, of course, one should never forget that he was acting in a professional capacity and not the informal one of friendship. One must always keep that in mind.

For the next month, Miss Falkenhagen read and read, and made copious notes on the index cards. She recorded all those sentences and paragraphs that seemed to her to be of exceptional value, but also the things that seemed to her pretentious or affected – and how many there were! In writing, as in life, honesty was the best policy, but also rare.

Her notebooks filled surprisingly quickly, and she soon needed others. She therefore had the impression that she was making very good progress.

The month between appointments with Dr Brown also went quickly. After a brief enquiry as to how she was feeling, Dr Brown asked her how the book was progressing.

'Very well,' said Miss Falkenhagen, again not without a slight twinge of conscience. 'Things have become very clear now. Everything has fallen into place.'

'Excellent,' said Dr Brown. 'I can't wait to read the first chapter.'

His obvious sincerity, which should have pleased Miss Falkenhagen, somehow gave her a slight chill through the heart.

'I am not sure,' she said, 'whether I should show anyone any of it until it is completed. Fragments can give a misleading impression, especially when there is an overall design. With all due respect to you, Dr Brown, of course, because naturally I would value your opinion very highly.'

'Oh, I quite understand,' said Dr Brown. And then they discussed a little (and in general) the relation of a part of a literary work to the whole. Once again the upshot was that Miss Falkenhagen should return in a month's time.

During those four weeks, Miss Falkenhagen could not disguise from herself that she had now read a number of memoirs, that each of them was different, that there was no absolute formula to be followed, and that therefore no further reading could really help her. She was now, in a manner of speaking, on her own: it was time really to begin.

She cleared the table, but that did not take long because in fact she was very tidy anyway. She took a new notebook and opened it, folding back its cover with almost ceremonial care. It was a lined notebook, with twenty-four lines per page. On average, with writing of her size, there would be ten words per line, that is to say, two hundred and forty words per page. And since the notebook had a hundred and twenty pages, that would mean, when she filled it, twenty-eight thousand, eight hundred words (you could expect the girls at the office to do a sum like that in their heads, not with the education, so-called, that they'd received).

That meant, of course, that her memoir would have to fill two, or perhaps two and a half, such notebooks. You could hardly expect people to pay good money for a book of less than fifty thousand words: famous authors might get away with it, but not someone completely unknown, as yet, to the public, like Miss Falkenhagen. Even a swastika on the cover would not make up for unacceptable slimness. Books should, of course, be exactly as long as their content warrants, neither longer nor shorter; but one should not disguise from oneself the imperatives of the market-place. Besides, fifty thousand words was not so very much: it was considerably fewer (not less: to have used the word 'less' here would have been the kind of grammatical solecism that the girls in the office might have made) - fewer than a thousand words per year she had lived, that is to say fewer than three per day. Surely no one in the world had lived so insignificant a life that its relation was worth fewer than three words per day, let alone Miss Falkenhagen, who had nearly seen Hitler and narrowly missed presenting him with flowers?

The lined blank page stared up at her – was it invitation or reproach? Silly to think of it like that, for dead objects like a page of paper did not have intentions or feelings. Miss Falkenhagen took up her pen.

She wrote the words 'I was born in' and then stopped. Surely they were too trite, though undoubtedly they would be true once she appended the date and place of her birth. But they might give the reader the impression that he was reading a birth certificate or other official document rather than a memoir. Compare it with (just to take a book at random) the first words of Edmund Blunden's memoir of the First World War, *Undertones of War*. They were, 'I was not anxious to go.' Go where? The reader's interest was piqued at once, one couldn't help but read on. Not even a swastika on the cover would save a book whose first sentence failed to engage the reader's attention, for no one bought a book without reading the first sentence.

The problem was that she had already those trite words, and thus soiled the page. She could, of course, scratch them out, but surely the first page of her manuscript should be word-perfect, without alterations? It was unrealistic to expect the whole manuscript to be without deletions, insertions and the like, but a first page ought to display something like a rush of inspiration. The page would have to go.

She tore it out carefully: someone such as she, who had lived through the destruction of whole cities, respected the least of inanimate objects because she knew what their total absence was like: unlike the spoilt flibbertigibbets that she worked with. But, neat and careful though she was, the torn edge of the page she had removed was still slightly visible in places, ragged and uneven. This was disturbing: you couldn't write perfect words on an imperfect page. Miss Falkenhagen had therefore to pull out the corresponding page which formed the second half of the sheet of the tied-in paper. That meant that the book was now four pages short of one hundred and twenty and that, instead of having twenty-eight thousand eight hundred words when filled, it would have twenty-seven thousand seven hundred and sixty. That, of course, hardly mattered; still Miss Falkenhagen felt uneasy at writing her memoir in notebooks of uneven length. She did not know where this uneasiness came from, but then, who does know from what source emerge his feelings?

The page in front of her was pristine once more, and her pen hovered over it, as if possessing a physical power of itself to remain in the air. Miss Falkenhagen thought hard: she needed a really striking opening sentence, something as memorable as the first words of Anna Karenina. She could take her time over it, because once it came, the rest would flow much more easily, as with the contents of a bottle whose neck was blocked with dried up sauce, say, and then suddenly unblocked.

Then she had it. 'Once I nearly met Hitler.' That, surely, was as good as a swastika on the cover. But then she began to have doubts. True, it was arresting; but might it not be thought ridiculous – that the high point of someone's life, and her sole claim to attention, being that she nearly met someone, but didn't quite meet? Besides, everything else afterwards might seem like an anti-climax. A first line should be good, but not so good that it put everything else in the shade.

On the other hand, it struck her as so good that she was reluctant to let it go. She could see how she might continue: for example, by recounting how it was that she nearly came to meet Hitler. But then her narrative would not be a strictly chronological one, and it would need more thought about its structure than she had so far given it. Well, there was no hurry; she would sleep on it. Often one's mind sorted out things by itself, as it were, without one having to think about it. The tip of the tongue phenomenon was like that: you tried and tried to remember something that you knew that you knew, but failed miserably, until you gave up and thought about something else, when hey presto! it came to you. The structure of a book could be like that, too. After all, some of the greatest authors had probably not been all that intelligent; they had simple possessed a powerful and accomplished subconscious.

And true enough, next day Miss Falkenhagen, or her subconscious, had taken the decision. 'Once I nearly met Hitler' it would be. And afterwards, it was just as she thought: it was like the liquid pouring from a bottle whose neck had been cleared of a blockage. What she wrote seemed to her to be very good.

Until, that is, she read it the next day. How she could ever have thought it remotely readable, let alone good, now puzzled her. Even making allowances for the fact that she had written it out of her memories, and therefore knew in advance everything that it said, it struck her as dull and uninteresting. Although she knew the English language well – none better, in fact – and her vocabulary was extensive (she made a point of looking up any unfamiliar word in the dictionary and committing it to memory by writing it down and testing herself later in the day) all her similes and metaphors came out hackneyed and lifeless. Of course, not every line could glitter: those writers who tried to be witty all the time soon grew tiresome to the reader, even if they succeeded; but still one needed sometimes to lift one's words from the realm of the conventional and the expected.

There was no choice, alas, but to start again, keeping nothing but the first sentence. This time, because she had already written so much, she had to tear twelve pages out of the notebook, which left only a hundred and four pages and the notebook palpably thinner than the others. She therefore discarded it – though it could still be used for other purposes – and took another. But that left her with one fewer in reserve, and she thought that she ought not to start writing again until she had replenished her stock. If she made a similar mistake in the new notebook, after all, she would be left with just one. Unfortunately, the shops were now closed, and she wouldn't have time to go to them for a couple of days to come. She therefore satisfied herself with writing 'Once I nearly met Hitler' in the new book, knowing that these five words, at least, would not need to be altered.

She was relieved to have a couple of days off from writing. It was hard work, writing, perhaps harder than she had suspected. The beginning of any book was bound to be difficult, more difficult than any other part of a book, and so she did not begrudge herself a few days' rest.

By the time her next appointment with Dr Brown came round, she had added another sentence to the manuscript: 'I will tell you how this came about.' Simple, unegotistical (the reproach of egotism being possible to level at any memoirist) and establishing a tone of honesty.

Dr Brown asked her how she was.

'Very well, thank you,' she replied.

'You look a little drawn to me,' said Dr Brown.

'Perhaps I've picked up a virus. There's one going about the office.'

Dr Brown seemed satisfied with that. He asked her how the book was going.

'Slowly,' she said. 'I want to get it right, word-perfect, first time.'

Dr Brown said there were two types of writer: those who wrote impulsively, torrentially as it were, and then corrected what they had written, and those like Miss Falkenhagen, who took minute care so that their first draft could and should be their last.

He fixed their next appointment for a month's time.

On the way home, Miss Falkenhagen began to wonder whether Dr Brown was quite such a good doctor after all. In fact, she began to be irritated by him. There was something glib about him, shallow. He hadn't enough experience of life for a job like the one he was doing, he hadn't known tragedy. It was obvious that he came from a decent family, he had probably gone through life like a hot knife through butter. Furthermore, he didn't know as much as he pretended about literature and the way it was created. He talked about it as if it were the same as revising for an exam and all that was necessary was a little self-discipline and firmness with yourself. Had he not heard of inspiration? Miss Falkenhagen supposed that medical studies were inclined to make you literal-minded and unimaginative. Was there not an old proverb, 'Where there are three physicians, there are two atheists?' Miss Falkenhagen was not religious herself, but despised the facile, know-all certitudes of those who had studied a little science.

She did not attend her next appointment with Dr Brown. This surprised him a little, even though he was quite accustomed to patients in general failing to attend, because Germans were punctilious in such matters. Still, everyone makes mistakes and forgets sometimes. Dr Brown sent Miss Falkenhagen another appointment through the post for two weeks' time.

She missed that appointment as well. It was very strange: someone dressed as neatly as she, especially in these casual times, was likely to be almost obsessional in her conduct. He sent her yet another appointment.

This, too, she failed to keep. Dr Brown dictated a letter to her general practitioner, informing him that as she had now missed three appointments in succession at the Mary Lamb Mental Wellness Centre, and had not contacted the clinic with an explanation, she was being discharged from follow-up. As he signed the letter, Dr Brown felt a slight unease.

A few days later, he received at telephone call from Miss Falkenhagen's general practitioner, the one who suggested that she came to see him.

'I thought you ought to know,' he said, 'that Miss Falkenhagen has died.'

'Has died?' repeated Dr Brown. Suicide, he thought? Suicide was to psychiatrists what dying on the table was to surgeons. It gives you a lot of trouble, quite apart from the tragedy of it.

'Yes, about three weeks ago.'

'What of?'

'Pneumonia. She was found dead in bed. The funny thing was that she didn't call anyone for help.'

- 2 -
The Proper Procedure

WHEN THEY CAME to take screaming Miss Budd away, they allowed her a few minutes to collect her things. They could hear her banging about upstairs for a time, but the ambulance men knew that she was not trying to escape. Seventy-five year-old ladies, however mad they are, do not jump from windows to avoid capture, unlike sane young men who will do anything to avoid authority.

Miss Budd came back downstairs with a bulging plastic carrier bag. The ambulance men were astonished by her appearance. They had heard that she had so terrified her neighbours that they had demanded that something be done about her. But how could anyone so small and frail have caused so much trouble? True, she had a slightly wild look, with glittering eyes and spikes of hair, not yet entirely white, sticking up like quills from her scalp. But she was not so much bird-like as bird-sized, and seemed to have desiccated to the absolute minimum compatible with life. Surely, then, she had been more a nuisance than a threat, with her constant imprecations and banging on the walls with her stick for hours on end? No one could seriously believe that she was dangerous, as the neighbours had claimed she was, exaggerating merely to get the attention of the authorities.

The ambulance men smiled at one another ironically.

'Come on, Lil,' one of them said, coaxing Miss Budd out of

the front door.

She was completely compliant, as is a man who recognises the inevitability of his own execution.

It was a short drive to the hospital. Miss Budd had never been there before, but she displayed little interest in her surroundings as the ambulance men guided her along the corridors, deserted at that time of night. At least there was nothing wrong with her walking, or mobility as it said on the paperwork that the men were carrying.

They reached the ward. All three of them stood for a time like people waiting to be seated at a restaurant; then they were approached by an unnaturally fat young woman, not in uniform, with a small stud in her nose.

'Lilly Budd for you,' said one of the ambulance men.

'Couldn't you've brought her earlier?' she said. 'I'm the only one on duty now.'

The ambulance men were not put out; they were used to this exasperated reception. It would have been just the same whatever time they had brought her; there was no convenient time to arrive.

'We've had lots of emergencies,' one of them said.

'All right,' said the nurse, not believing them, on the contrary believing that they had arranged to arrive now just to make her life difficult. 'You can leave her to me.'

The ambulance men left without saying goodbye to Miss Budd. It was late, and they were tired.

'Well, Lil,' said the nurse turning to Miss Budd, 'what have we been up to, then?'

Miss Budd did not answer. In fact, she did not know what the nurse was talking about. She had only done what anyone else would have done in the circumstances, that is to say when their neighbours were pumping poison gas through the walls and shouting abuse day and night, preventing them from sleeping and making them feel ill.

'Follow me,' said the nurse, adding, 'No problems walking, I suppose,' half a statement and half a question. She led Miss Budd into an office with glass walls through which you could see passages leading to the bedrooms. In the foreground was a kind of sitting room, with low armchairs and some plastic-topped tables.

'We've got some paperwork to do before you go to bed,' said the nurse as she sat down at a desk. Miss Budd was still standing, her hand clutching her carrier bag.

'Why don't you sit down,' said the Nurse, and Miss Budd sat down gingerly, as if the invitation were a trap. Once she was in her chair, she found herself looking up at the nurse.

'Now then, said the nurse, drawing some papers towards her on the desk in front of her, 'I've just got a few questions…'

Miss Budd shifted slightly in her seat.

'You are Lilly Budd, of 47 William Cobbett Tower?' asked the nurse. 'We don't want any silly mistakes.' She laughed at the thought of silly mistakes: the wrong medicine for the wrong patients, that kind of thing. The effects of silly mistakes could be very peculiar.

Miss Budd did not answer and the nurse repeated her question. This time she nodded her assent.

'Date of birth?' asked the nurse. The details had already been given over the telephone by the doctor who had arranged for Miss Budd's admission, but there was nothing like having it from the person herself. It was also a test of how far gone the patient might be, if she couldn't answer.

Miss Budd took a long time over it, and the nurse eventually read out the date the doctor had given and asked Miss Budd whether it was right.

Miss Budd only muttered or mumbled her answers to subsequent questions, which – because of the late hour – the nurse took as assent to her own answers to her own questions. It would have taken all night, probably, to elicit genuine answers.

'Now I've got to make a list of your property,' said the nurse.

So saying, she came round from the desk and bent down to take Miss Budd's carrier bag from her. But Miss Budd withdrew the bag from her reach with surprising speed and dexterity.

'Now don't be silly,' said the nurse. 'I'm only trying to make a list, I'm not trying to take anything. We have to make a list of everyone's property.'

By now Miss Budd was clutching her bag to her bony chest. The nurse tried to be reasonable, and to make her see reason.

'If we don't make a list and something goes missing we won't have a record of it, will we?'

This evident fact did not strike Miss Budd very forcefully, for she still clutched the bag to her as if for dear life, and the nurse had to admit to herself that the problem with patients, sometimes, was that they were just not very bright.

'I'll just make a little list of what you have and hand everything straight back to you,' said the nurse, in a last ditch effort at persuasion. 'There's nothing to be afraid of, I'm not going to steal anything.'

Miss Budd stared around her in a distracted fashion.

'Right,' said the nurse firmly. 'We haven't got all night. There are other patients who need attention, you know.' And she ripped the bag from Miss Budd's bony grasp.

'There, that wasn't so bad now, was it?' said the nurse, as if she had just finished an examination of a child, or vaccinated it.

Miss Budd accepted the loss of her bag as a *fait accompli* and the nurse returned behind her desk, on whose top she now placed it.

'What have we got here?' she asked, lifting a crumpled white night-dress from the bag and suspending it in the air between her thumb and forefinger, and then bringing it close to her and giving it a sniff.

'Not very clean,' she said. 'You've been letting yourself go, Lilly, haven't you?'

'I been too... They won't let me,' said Miss Budd, in the clearest voice she had used up till now.

'Never mind,' said the nurse, dropping it on to the floor and glad to see it go. 'We'll get it cleaned. You won't need it here. We'll give you a fresh one to wear. That would be better, wouldn't it?'

Miss Budd said nothing, so the nurse took it that she was pleased; after all, who wouldn't want her washing done, and for nothing?

She rummaged further in the bag and found two further

items of clothing that she held up as if in an act of public accusation.

'Now what are these?' she said, dropping them very quickly. 'They're filthy. We'll have them washed too – perhaps they'll need more than one wash. Maybe they should even be thrown away. We can get you some new clothes. And you probably need a wash too. We can't have you going to bed like that, can we Lil?'

The nurse put her hand back into the bag without looking.

'What's this?' she exclaimed.

She drew out some bank notes, a whole fistful of them in fact. Then she put her hand in again, peered into the bag and tipped the contents out on to the top of the desk. Money emerged like confetti, a small fortune, or at least more than two or three months' wages.

'What did you bring all this for?' asked the nurse, a little angry that a little old woman, obviously unqualified and not very clever, should have so much cash. 'You don't need money here.'

Miss Budd muttered something about savings and it not being safe to give the money to anybody else, but so indistinctly and apologetically (it seemed to the nurse) that she must have had a bad conscience about it.

'You've really landed me with a serious problem,' said the nurse. 'What to do with all this money. Normally, it would go to the office, but the office is closed at this time of night.'

Miss Budd offered to keep it with her but the nurse was horrified by the suggestion.

'Patient's aren't allowed to have more than five pounds cash on them,' she said. 'For obvious reasons,' she added.

The reasons were not clear to Miss Budd. She said something about it being her money.

'Nobody's saying that it isn't,' said the nurse sharply. 'That's not the question. The point is that you can't keep it here with you. I'll have to count it and then look after it until the morning when it can go down to the office.'

It took her a long time to count it because she lost her thread two or three times and had to start again.

'I'm a nurse, not a bank clerk,' she said.

At last she came to the total: two thousand three hundred and sixty-five pounds. She sucked air through her teeth and then found some rubber bands in the drawer of the desk with which to tie up the money in little piles.

'You'll have to sign a receipt,' she said, waving a piece of paper at her.

Miss Budd said something about not having her glasses with her, which irritated the nurse because she thought it was an attempt at an excuse to avoid signing.

'You'll just have to do the best you can,' she said, leading, or more like pulling, Miss Budd to the edge of the desk and guiding her hand, into which she had put a pen, on to the receipt. Miss Budd made a weak, spidery mark.

'Good,' said the nurse. 'And now perhaps we can get on and get you to bed.'

Miss Budd made a quick recovery, thanks to some little blue pills which she had little choice but to take. When asked about the poisoned gas and the neighbours' insults, she laughed nervously and said they had stopped now; perhaps the neighbours had thought better of what they were doing.

The doctor tried to get her to say that there never had been any poison gas or insults, but Miss Budd remained silent.

'Well,' said the doctor cheerily, 'the main thing is that they've stopped.' He told her that she would be going home soon, and she was pleased. Winicott Ward was not very nice.

The very next day, about half past five in the evening, when it was dark outside, a nurse – this one with a rose tattooed on her neck – came to Miss Budd's bed, where she was resting, with a smile on her face.

'Good news, Lil,' she said. 'You're going home now.'

Since Miss Budd had never wanted to come in the first place, she was not overjoyed; the nurse was disappointed at her lack of gratitude. All Miss Budd said was:

'How am I going to get there?'

'Transport's all arranged and on its way,' said the nurse. 'It'll be here in a quarter of an hour.'

'Couldn't I go tomorrow?' said Miss Budd. 'It's dark.'

'We need the bed,' said the nurse with asperity, as if Miss Budd were intent on denying treatment to the newcomer for whom the bed was needed. 'Besides, we can't cancel the transport now. It's on its way. You'll have to change out of your hospital clothes.'

The nurse fetched Miss Budd's clothes, which had been cleaned but not pressed.

'Quick,' she said. 'We haven't much time.'

Miss Budd changed her clothes under the eye of the nurse, who feared both deliberate error and delay. A telephone sounded and the nurse went to answer it. She returned after a few moments, putting her head round the door.

'Transport's here,' she said.

'Quick,' said another nurse who had joined her. 'We don't want to keep it waiting, or it'll go.' She came in and cupped her hand round Miss Budd's elbow to ease her out of the room.

'What about my money?' asked Miss Budd, trying to stop in her tracks.

'What money?' said the nurse, applying a little more pressure to her elbow and pushing her forward. Did the old woman actually expect to be paid to go home? The more you did for people, the more they expected.

'The money what I had when I come in here,' said Miss Budd.

'I don't know anything about that,' said the nurse. 'I wasn't on duty then.'

'Only I came in with a lot of money,' said Miss Budd. 'The nurse took it off me and said she sent it to the office because of thieves. I want it back before I go.'

'It's too late now,' said the nurse. 'You should've mentioned it before. The office is closed now.'

'What can I do, then?' asked Miss Budd. 'I want my money.'

'Well, you won't need it tonight, will you Lilly? I mean, you're not going to a night-club, I don't suppose. You can come back tomorrow and get it when the office opens.'

'I don't know where the office is,' said Miss Budd.

Where did she think it was? The far side of the moon? The hospital was a small one.

'Downstairs, of course,' said the nurse, now seriously worried about the transport. Sometimes it wouldn't wait, and then there would be a real problem. There would be more patients on the ward than beds to put them in. The nurse applied even more pressure to Miss Budd's elbow to hurry her along.

Miss Budd returned to the hospital the following morning. The Administrator's Office was not easy to find, for though the hospital was small, it was big enough for it to have a warren of corridors on the ground floor, dark with closed office doors. Mostly the corridors were deserted; when someone emerged from an office, he was so obviously intent on his own business that Miss Budd dared not obtrude. For his part, the person in the corridor assumed that Miss Budd was merely a patient that had wandered from one of the wards, and it was the duty of the ward staff to retrieve her: not his. Office staff could not interfere in clinical matters, if for no other reason than that they were not insured to do so.

By dint of wandering for several minutes, however, Miss Budd eventually found a door that was open. The office inside was surprisingly light; it had a window practically the height of the wall, which alterations to the old fabric of the building had not blocked off. Seated at a desk was the Personal Assistant to the Administrator. Miss Budd entered timidly, not so much knocking on the open door as scraping it very slightly.

'I've come for my money,' she said.

'I'm sorry, I don't know who you are,' said the Personal Assistant. 'Who are you?'

'Lilly Budd.'

'I mean, what ward are you from?' Not that she really expected an answer, because when old people go wandering they know neither where they're going, nor where they've come from, not even where they were. It had been a mistake to give difficult names to the wards such as Aubrey Lewis or Mayer-Gross, because they confused the confused even further. Why not just

Ward One, Two and so forth? When she had asked the Administrator, however, he said that numbers sounded impersonal. Better the name of famous psychiatrists of old.

'I've come for the money what I brought with me when I come in here,' said Miss Budd.

'You're allowed only five pounds in your possession while you're a patient,' said the Personal Assistant. 'Hospital rules.'

'I'm not in the hospital no more,' said Miss Budd. 'I been sent home.'

'So why didn't you take your money with you when you went?'

'It was too late. They sent it down to the office.'

'Oh,' said the Personal Assistant, stretching out her exclamation as if into the distance. The light of recognition came into her eyes. 'You're not the patient who came into the hospital with more than two thousand pounds in a plastic bag, are you?'

'Yes, I'm Lilly Budd.'

'Ha! ha! ha!' laughed the Personal Assistant. Her mirth had a slight ring of exasperation in it. 'Did you think we weren't going to feed you, then?'

'Only they said that I should ask the Administrator to get it back,' said Miss Budd.

The Personal Assistant was a little put out that Miss Budd had not even noticed her little sally; that's what it was, of course, to have a one-track mind, or no sense of humour. Perhaps it was a lack of sense of humour that led to people having to come into hospitals such as this.

'Do you have an appointment to see him?' asked the Personal Assistant.

'No, I never,' said Miss Budd.

The Personal Assistant frowned. Really, people were the limit. They expected to be attended to the moment they felt like it. They concluded that, just because they had nothing much to do, and therefore no schedule, no one else had much to do and no schedule. They probably thought that hospitals ran themselves.

'I'll give you one then,' said the Personal Assistant, as if conferring a valuable benefit upon Miss Budd. 'Unfortunately, he's away next week. He's at Headquarters for a strategic planning meeting. I'm sure you'll appreciate just how important that is, our whole future depends on it. But you can come the week after. I don't suppose it matters to you which day of the week?'

Miss Budd did not look like, nor was she, the kind of person with a busy schedule.

'How about Wednesday, then?' said the Personal Assistant. 'At eleven forty-five. Is that all right for you?

Miss Budd opened her mouth but no sound came out.

'Good, that's all right then,' said the Personal Assistant. 'It's fixed. I'll write it down for you so you won't forget.'

She handed Miss Budd a slip of paper.

Miss Budd must have misunderstood, because she went to the hospital on the following Wednesday instead of Wednesday the week following. The Personal Assistant was rather put out, irritated, by this confusion, because she had done everything possible to avoid it arising. She could hardly have made herself clearer. It was as if what she had said about the Strategic Planning Meeting – the SPM – had gone in one of Miss Budd's ears and come straight out of the other. It was not that they – the SPMs – took place often, not more than two or three times a year. This time they were even discussing the closure of the hospital because it was uneconomic. There was obviously a crisis on and this woman couldn't even remember which Wednesday she was supposed to come.

So Miss Budd, after what amounted to a scolding, came back the following Wednesday. She arrived half an hour early and waited in the entrance hall to the hospital, where there was somewhere to sit down. She watched the minute hand of the clock on the wall jerk forward towards her appointed time.

'Ah, Miss Budd,' said the Personal Assistant when she saw her as she appeared outside the door to her room. 'Bad news, I'm afraid. The Administrator's been called away. These things are unavoidable, though I agree it's a nuisance, even for me. It's all a matter of finance these days, that's all they're worried about.'

Miss Budd seemed uncomprehending about this situation.

'I've come about my money,' she said.

'But I've told you, the Administrator's away. But I'll tell you what I'll do, just to help you. I'll bring forward your next appointment with him to this Friday. How's that? I'll make sure he squeezes you in, though he's very busy on Fridays. Sometimes you just have to be firm with him.'

Miss Budd arrived on Friday morning. The Personal Assistant told her the Administrator was running a little late this morning, but that he would definitely see her today.

'You could go to the patients' canteen and have a cup of tea,' she said. 'He'll be back in half an hour.'

Instead of going to the canteen, Miss Budd hovered round the corner, out of sight. The Administrator was as good as the Personal Assistant's word, however. Suddenly he burst from his office through a door into her room. He was a tall man with slicked back hair and a tan despite the less than sunny weather.

'Ah, Miss Budd, Miss Budd,' he said. 'We meet at last. Do come in.'

And he guided her into his room like the head-waiter of an expensive restaurant guiding a celebrity to his table. His progress across the floor seemed frictionless.

'Please sit down,' he said.

Miss Budd sat down in a steel-framed chair, cold to the touch, with a leather seat slung across that swayed with any movement and made her feel a little sick. The room was large, with heavy silk curtains, and on the large desk in front of her was apparatus whose purpose or function she could not guess.

'Before we begin,' said the Administrator, sitting on the opposite side of the desk, 'there are just one or two formalities we have to go through. I suppose you've brought some ID with you?'

'ID?' said Miss Budd vacantly. 'What's that? I've come for my money.'

'Identification,' said the Administrator. 'So that we know that you are who you say you are.'

'I'm Lilly Budd,' said Miss Budd.

'Yes,' said the Administrator, laughing pleasantly, 'you and I know that, but not everyone might. We have to be able to prove it. Due diligence and all that, especially these days.'

'Jew who?' said Miss Budd.

'We have to be careful, Miss Budd. Someone could impersonate you. Pretend to be Miss Budd who wasn't.'

'But I'm Lilly Budd, I always been Lilly Budd, ever since I was born.'

'Yes, I know you have,' said the Administrator. 'But let's suppose someone came in here claiming to be Lilly Budd who wasn't, and then we just handed the money over, we wouldn't have a leg to stand on, would we? What would you say then?'

Miss Budd was silent and the Administrator took it that she was appalled at the thought which had never occurred to her before.

'And let's face it, Miss Budd, two thousand pounds is a lot of money to hand out to the wrong person. It's not tuppence ha'penny, is it? No. If we lost your money, you'd hold us responsible, wouldn't you, and rightly so. So we have to be careful, as I'm sure you'd be the first to agree.'

Still Miss Budd was silent.

'So you see, we need proof of your identity before we can proceed.'

'What's that?' said Miss Budd.

'Proof of identity?' repeated the Administrator, half-disbelieving. Were there still people like this in the world? 'You know, something like a passport or a driving licence.'

Again Miss Budd was silent. Abroad meant nothing to her, and she was more likely to be run over by a car than to drive one.

'Or a gas bill,' said the Administrator, descending to Miss Budd's level. 'Even a rent book. Normally we ask for two documents, but in your case I think one will do. There,' he said, getting up from his chair on the other side of the desk, and coming round to Miss Budd's side, 'just pop along with a gas bill and we'll soon have everything sorted out.'

To his surprise, Miss Budd did not get up. Instead she remained seated as if fixed to the chair.

'I just came for the money what I brought when I come in hospital,' she said.

The Administrator often wished he was in charge of a hospital in an area with a more intelligent population.

'Didn't my P.A. tell you to bring some I.D. with you?' he asked.

'What's that?' asked Miss Budd.

'P.A.? Personal Assistant.' Miss Budd looked bemused. 'Used to be secretary,' said the Administrator, raising his voice to overcome Miss Budd's evident slight loss of hearing (but not loud enough for the Personal Assistant to hear, he hoped). 'Writing letters, answering the phone, that kind of thing. Anyway, didn't she tell you?'

'No she never,' said Miss Budd.

The face of the Administrator darkened a little. He flung open the door from his to the Personal Assistant's room.

'Miss Budd says you didn't tell her to bring any I.D. with her,' said the Administrator, with anger in his voice.

'I think I did,' said the Personal Assistant. 'Perhaps I didn't. I thought it was obvious.'

There was no mistaking the instructions this time, however, and Miss Budd returned two days later with her gas bill and her pension book, as well as a letter addressed to her, admittedly a few years old, from her second cousin Robert, with who she had since lost touch and who might even have died.

'That seems to be in order,' said the Administrator when he looked them over, remarking to himself on Robert's bad spelling and leaving open the possibility that some defect might be found in this evidence a little later. Oddly enough, he had had to be reminded by the Personal Assistant as to who Miss Budd was.

'Can I have my money now, then?' asked Miss Budd.

'Hold your horses, Miss Budd, hold your horses,' he said, laughing mirthlessly. 'Rome wasn't built in a day.'

'Only I'd like it now,' she said.

Surely she couldn't actually need it now, thought the Administrator. You only had to look at her to know that she was a hoarder rather than a spender: probably she never threw anything out, and he wouldn't be surprised (if he went to her home) to discover that she kept even piles of old newspapers.

'There's something I have to tell you, Miss Budd,' said the Administrator. 'We don't have your money in our possession at the moment. The fact is that when you came to hospital with so much cash – and I remind you that it was not at our instigation that you did so – you put us in a bit of a quandary.'

'A what?' said Miss Budd.

'A quandary.' Seeing Miss Budd's blank face, the Administrator realised that the problem was not her hearing but her comprehension. 'A quandary,' he repeated, 'a dilemma.'

'What's that?' said Miss Budd.

'A dilemma?' The Administrator was quite busy enough without having to be a walking dictionary to the ignorant aged as well. 'It's a choice between two alternatives neither of which is quite right,' he said.

The Administrator drew himself up to his full height. That wasn't a bad definition, he thought, considering that it was off the cuff and he that had never given it a moment's thought before. Miss Budd, however, was not visibly impressed: clearly, purely intellectual pleasures were not hers.

'Where's my money, then?' she asked.

'That's precisely what I was going to tell you,' said the Administrator. 'You see, our office safe is a very small one. I've written to the Chief Executive to tell him that, in my opinion, we could do with a bigger one. Any novice could break into the one we have. But you know what it is, Miss Budd, in these times of financial retrenchment. I don't need to tell you that all expenditure on non-essentials is the first thing to be cut at such a time. And I'm afraid that a larger safe, such as we could keep patients' valuables in, safely as it were, falls into the category of non-essential.'

Miss Budd said nothing.

'Besides,' said the Administrator, 'there is the question of insurance. As I'm sure you know, this is a high crime area. That means that insurance on removable valuables – and there's nothing more removable or valuable than cash, is there? – is prohibitively expensive. I'm sure that you appreciate that we couldn't risk holding your cash without insurance, don't you?'

The Administrator waited for a reply, but Miss Budd said nothing.

'Don't you?' repeated the Administrator, but to no effect. 'So putting the two things together,' he resumed in the absence of any response, 'the lack of space in the safe, and the prohibitive cost of insurance, we really had no choice but to send your money to Headquarters for safe-keeping.'

'Where are they?' asked Miss Budd.

'Oh, that really doesn't matter,' said the Administrator. 'At any rate for your purposes,' he added. 'Of course, we'll get the money back for you and deliver it to you. We don't want to put you as our client to any trouble. But you see, not only is Headquarters in a better area where there is less crime, but they are equipped there for this kind of situation. They have a much bigger and better safe. A safer safe, if you like.'

His laugh was more like a cough.

'So when can I have my money?' asked Miss Budd.

'Soon, very soon, Miss Budd. I've already contacted Headquarters about it, and they've given a positive response. They're fully aware of the situation. Your money should be here any day now.'

'When can I have it, then?' she asked.

'I've just said, Miss Budd, as soon as it arrives, as soon as it arrives.' Really, did she think that anyone was trying to do her out of her money, a paltry sum, after all, in the wider scheme of things? Perhaps she was still so paranoid that she should never have been released from hospital.

'When will that be?' asked Miss Budd.

'A few days, a few days. And now if you'll excuse me, Miss Budd, I have a hospital to run.'

Miss Budd came back three days later. The Personal Assistant made a great show of looking through the Administrator's diary before announcing that, as she did not have an appointment, he was not expecting her.

'But I have a window of opportunity next Tuesday,' she said. 'It's very short, I'm afraid, just ten minutes, but that should do, shouldn't it? I mean, you haven't got much to discuss, have you?' A small explosion of air, almost like a laugh, emerged from her mouth. 'And don't be late, otherwise he won't have time to see you.'

From then on Miss Budd began to haunt the hospital. She became like a ghostly, flitting presence, never quite present, never quite absent, appearing suddenly at the Personal Assistant's door, sometimes several times a day. It began to get on the Personal Assistant's nerves. She who had an almost religious reverence for the authority of the Administrator nevertheless plucked up the courage one day to tell him that he had to do something about Miss Budd because she – the Personal Assistant – couldn't stand the constant dumb reproach of that woman much longer. And yet she had the impression that the Administrator, so tall, so capable, so efficient, was actually trying to avoid meeting Miss Budd. Once, for example, he burst out of his office and rushed past her without saying anything at all to her, though he must surely have seen her. Another time, when he could hardly have passed her without pushing her out of the way, he pretended that he was glad that he had met her.

'Ah, Miss Budd,' he said expansively, his hand extended to shake hers. 'Good to see you, good to see you.'

Miss Budd, who had no social graces, did not shake the proffered hand, only looked at it, and he returned it to his side.

'What can I do for you this morning?' he asked sunnily.

'Only I've come for my money,' said Miss Budd.

'Oh!' said the Administrator, as if his memory had just been jogged. 'Of course you have, of course you have.'

'Can I have it now?' asked Miss Budd.

'Ah,' said the Administrator, dragging out the word to increase its meaning and delay a little. 'There's been a slight hitch,

I'm afraid. You see, the Treasurer didn't want to keep so much cash on the premises, even though it was perfectly safe. A matter of principle, really. So the money was paid into a bank account.'

'Only I been waiting long enough,' said Miss Budd.

'Of course you have, we all agree,' said the Administrator. 'And I sympathise, I honestly really do. The problem, however, is that the person who paid the money into the bank, whoever it was (and I promise you that I'll try to find out who it was) paid it into the wrong account. Instead of paying it into the General Purposes – petty cash is what you'll know it by – he or she (I mustn't say these days that it was probably a she) paid it into the Capital Expenditure account. Of course, you know what that means.'

Miss Budd gave no sign of it.

'No?' said the Administrator, surprised. 'Well, money that is in the General Purposes account, only up to a certain amount of course, but two thousand pounds is well within those limits, can be withdrawn on the signature of only one responsible signatory, but cheques drawn on the Capital Expenditure account have to be countersigned by the Treasurer himself who, I'm afraid, Miss Budd, is off work sick – or it may be at a conference, I'm not absolutely sure. I think it has something to do with his bowels, though.'

'So when can I have my money? asked Miss Budd.

'As soon as the Treasurer returns to work,' said the Administrator. 'And that won't be long now. I know him of old: wild horses wouldn't normally keep him off work.'

Two weeks passed and Miss Budd returned to the hospital. The Personal Assistant was all smiles.

'I think the Administrator's got good news for you,' she said. 'I won't spoil it for you by telling you what it is.'

She called the Administrator on the intercom.

'Miss Budd's here to see you,' she said.

'I'll be out in a moment,' came the reply.

After a few minutes, the door burst open and the Administrator almost hurled himself out. He, too, was smiling broadly.

'Good news, Miss Budd, good news. We have your money now. Would you like to step into my office?'

The Administrator ushered Miss Budd once more into the room in which the award ceremony was to take place.

'First, Miss Budd, I'd like to thank you for your patience and understanding.'

'You got my money, then?' asked Miss Budd.

'Of course, of course,' said the Administrator. 'You didn't think we'd run off with it, did you?' He laughed at the idea. He pressed the intercom button on his desk.

'Could you come in here for a moment and act as a witness?' he asked the Personal Assistant.

The Personal Assistant entered and nodded a smile of recognition at Miss Budd.

'And now, Miss Budd, here is your money.'

The Administrator handed Miss Budd a slip of paper. It was a cheque.

Miss Budd looked from the Administrator to the Personal Assistant and back again.

'But where's my money?' she asked.

The Administrator, who had been expecting some sign of pleasure if not of gratitude, for the whole business had involved him in a lot of extra work (which he hardly needed, especially at this time of the year), was slightly irritated.

'That is your money, Miss Budd, that is your money. It's a cheque.'

'But I brought more than two thousand pound when I come in here,' she said.

'So you did, Miss Budd, so you did. We all agree. No one knows it better than I. I've been dealing with the consequences for weeks now. But that piece of paper you have in your hand, that cheque, Miss Budd, is for more than two thousand pounds. You're rich again!'

He laughed. Miss Budd looked blankly at the slip of paper.

'Two thousand, three hundred and fifty pounds,' said the Administrator. 'Exactly what you brought it, less fifteen pounds administration fee – a very poor hourly rate, let me tell you.' He laughed, and so did the Personal Assistant. Then he resumed. 'The Treasurer thought, and I must say that I agree with him, that it would be unsafe for a woman of your age to walking the streets with so much cash in her possession. That's why we're returning your money in the form of a cheque. It's so much safer.'

Then he changed his tone. He became brusque and businesslike.

'And now if you'll just sign this receipt. I'm afraid we're in a rush as usual.'

He pointed to another slip of paper on his desk.

'What do I do with it?' asked Miss Budd, holding up the cheque.

'Really, Miss Budd,' you can't expect me to tell you how to spend or invest your money. It's yours, after all, to do what you like with.'

He guided her firmly in the direction of the slip of paper on his desk and put a pen in her hand.

'Sign here,' he said, and Miss Budd, still unused to writing, made a spidery mark on the paper.

'Just as well we've got a witness,' said the Administrator, smiling. The Personal Assistant came forward to add her signature to the piece of paper.

The Administrator let out his breath with relief, as after an ordeal.

'It's over now, Miss Budd,' he said. 'All's well that ends well, as I always say.' Now he guided her towards the door.

'Goodbye, Miss Budd. Take care now.'

Half an hour later an old woman, ill-dressed, thin and wizened, collapsed in a busy shopping street not far from the hospital.

Some people walked round her, others stood and stared, some fussed ineffectually with her prostrate body. No one noticed the slip of paper that had fluttered away from her grasp as she fell to the ground.

'Quick,' someone said. 'Call an ambulance. We've got to get her to hospital.'

- 3 -
The Perfick Murder

VIRGINIA MCSTEPHEN was only ten years old when she was brought by her parents to England, but she never lost her accent.

They were respectable, hard-working, god-fearing and church-going people. They wanted to better themselves and give their daughter a better chance in life. They worked hard at their ill-paid jobs and saved money, putting it towards buying a little house of their own. At church on Sundays, Mrs McStephen, who was normally very self-controlled, wept and wailed a bit, publicly proclaimed herself a terrible sinner, writhed and twisted, spoke sometimes in tongues and, by the end of the service, felt she had been washed clean by the blood of Jesus. Her Sunday clothes, despite her writhings, remained extremely neat, a joy to the eye: her broad-brimmed hat, her snow-white gloves, her blue polka-dot dress. Mr McStephen was rather less ardent in his religion than his wife, and a few times in his married life he had girlfriends, whom his wife knew about and for which she forgave him. After all, it wasn't every man who went out to work day after day, year after year, and did not altogether squander the proceeds. One must count one's blessings and be thankful for small mercies.

Virginia did not turn out quite as Mr and Mrs McStephen (especially Mrs McStephen) had hoped, however. They wanted her to be something serious like a nurse, but at school she was more interested in lipstick and boys than in her work. Her only notion of bettering herself was to make herself more attractive to boys.

'You'll end up with nothing, girl,' said her mother to her repeatedly.

Virginia, who had developed a good line in cheek, said that she wasn't going to work for years just to buy a pokey little house like theirs.

'You want to live in a shack, then?' asked her mother.

No, a palace, thought Virginia, and flounced out.

Her taste in boys was bad. Solid attainments held no attraction for her. She preferred a flashing smile, a bit of a swagger and dashing words. She admired boys who did not work and yet from time to time appeared to have more money than they knew what to do with, and who bought, or at any rate brought, her things. She took it as a sign of success in life, though not in school, if a boy adorned himself with gold. An irregular existence was for her proof that a boy was a man and not a slave; not boring but good fun. A boy like that knew what life was really about.

There were many arguments about what time she came home at night. She seemed to want to be entirely nocturnal: day was for resting, night was for playing. There was therefore no time for work, and she sought none. She left school as soon as the law permitted, and she awaited her departure with impatience. The subjects in which she had excelled in her last two or three years were the application of mascara, gossip and smoking.

Her parents knew where it would all end and it did. A few months after her retirement from school, Virginia stopped going out at night and was sick in the mornings. Her mother, knowing perfectly well what it meant, asked her whether there was anything wrong, whether there was anything she wanted to tell her.

'No,' snapped Virginia, as though the questions were stupid.

A few days later, her mother was more direct.

'Who's the father?' she asked.

'Father?' sneered Virginia. 'Father of what? There ain't no father.'

'He's got to marry you whoever he is,' said her mother.

Virginia laughed derisively at the idea. Her mother did not understand. Things weren't like that any more. Besides, she couldn't really say who the father was; and none of the candidates for the position seemed eager to step forward and take it. Very much to the contrary.

'Wait till I tell your father,' said her mother.

'What's he gonna do about it?' asked Virginia contemptuously.

In fact, there was nothing to be done except wait for the birth. It was Mrs McStephen, not Virginia, who made the arrangements: bought the cot and baby clothes, rang for appointments with the doctor, and so forth. Virginia had stopped vomiting and resumed her social life; she seemed hardly interested in her own near future.

But eventually the pregnancy slowed her down, and then the baby was born. Mrs McStephen was torn between dismay and maternal feelings, the latter of which Virginia shared only intermittently. The baby was so sweet and helpless, and yet, all unknowing, had such a difficult life in front of her! Mrs McStephen didn't really approve of the name that Virginia chose for her, Waylene, a name that was purely whimsical and made up; but the christening went ahead anyway.

'What you gonna do now, Virginny,' asked Mr McStephen on the way home from the christening. Mrs McStephen was wiping away tears of shame because her close friend, Mrs Lee, had been there.

Virginia announced that she had obtained a flat from the council and that she would be moving in next week.

'You sure you can manage it, girl?' asked her mother.

What was there to manage? What did they take her for?

'You got any furniture?' asked Mr McStephen.

The council had seen to that, but the baby turned out to be a problem. Virginia loved playing with her, sometimes, but she was still young and could hardly be expected to stay within the four walls of her flat all the time. Fortunately, her mother was there to look after the baby whenever necessary, which became more and more often, especially once the baby began to walk, fall over things, and put her fingers in dangerous places. Before long, the baby was spending more time at her grandmother's, where she was more content in any case, than at her mother's. Outwardly her grandmother was angry at the imposition, but secretly she was pleased, even though she still went out to work and Virginia never had.

Then Virginia met the love of her life. She met him at about eleven o'clock one night while standing in the queue to get into a night club. He was about ten years older than she, and on his own. He told her he had just broken up with his girlfriend because she 'cheated on me.' Virginia was sympathetic and said she knew just how he felt, and then he asked her to keep his place in the queue for a moment while he went and saw someone. He returned very quickly with a hibiscus flower that he put in her hair. She laughed. Tropical flowers were not easy to obtain in the city in the middle of the night in the middle of winter, so that Virginia thought he must be a clever and resourceful man.

This he confirmed when she asked him where he got it.

'I know where you can get everything,' he said. 'Come on,' he added, taking her by the hand, 'we don't want to stand here for ever.'

He pulled her out of the queue and up to its head, which was presided over by a man who looked wider than most men are tall. He was dressed only in black and had a miniature microphone descending from an ear-piece to his mouth. It was he who decided who was admitted, in what order, and who was kept out. At that time, therefore, he was the most important man in the world for quite a number of people.

'Hi, man,' said Virginia's new companion.

The doorman looked at him first as if he might be some kind of buzzing insect, but then he recognised him.

'Hi, howyadooin,' he said, and the two men exchanged a closed fist greeting.

'Can you do something for us, man?' asked Virginia's companion.

'Sure, man,' said the doorman. 'You got it.'

There were a few mutters of discontent as he guided Virginia and her new companion through the club door but they were the impotent complaints of the vassals about their feudal lord. A glance from the doorman was enough to quell them.

Virginia was very impressed. It seemed that Dwayne – by now he had told her his name – really did know how to get whatever he wanted. He muscled his way to the bar and bought her a pink fizzy cocktail with some mint leaves in it, and some sugar round the edge of the glass, and Virginia thought she had landed on her feet to find such a man.

Before the night was over, they had decided to live together, at least when he wanted to. Dwayne said that he still had a place of his own that he wanted to keep; and though she never saw it, Virginia knew that it must have been true because he brought so little with him when he moved in. The rest of his stuff must obviously have been at his place. Besides, except for the first few weeks, he rarely stayed with her more than a few nights at a time, disappearing for another few nights without explanation. He had, after all, to go somewhere.

When he returned she sometimes asked him where he had been and what he had done, and he laughed and told her not to worry her pretty little head about it; if she insisted on knowing details he would grow angry and ask her whether she was the secret police or something, and threaten to leave her. This always worked; she inquired no further.

The first time he hit her was when she told him that she was pregnant. This was about three months after they had met. She had thought he would be pleased – was not a baby both a sign and a seal of love? – but he called her a whore and a bitch. He obviously thought that her pregnancy was a plot to entangle him and extract money from him; but if she thought that, she had another think coming to her. He wasn't a fool.

Not that he moved out altogether; indeed, he apologised to her. But his visits and overnight stays became fewer and farther between. When he did come, the sight of her pregnancy enraged him, as if it had nothing to do with him and another man had made her pregnant. He slapped her a few times and punched her, usually on the arms so that the bruises could be covered up, but once he aimed a kick at her stomach and she thought she would miscarry, but she didn't. He always apologised after he hit her, but told her it was her fault because he wasn't ready to settle down and he felt pressured. Then he would buy her some flowers, and fool around while presenting them to her to make her laugh. Virginia was angry, guilty, afraid and charmed.

Once she tried not to let him in when he arrived, but he broke in by a window (the flat was on the ground floor) and was then more aggressive than usual, putting his hand round her neck and accusing her of being a prostitute. She never tried to stop him again, and wasn't even sure whether she wanted to.

Dwayne was a little better after the baby was born and even evinced some pride in his offspring.

'He'll be the heavyweight champion,' he said, chucking the baby, now at Dwayne's insistence called Evander, under the chin.

One day, on visiting Evander and conferring on him a pair of bootees as if in fulfilment once and for all of an onerous contractual obligation, he let slip that Evander was his fifth child, two other boys and two girls. Perhaps that explained why he did not contribute very much to Evander's upkeep. He couldn't, at least not without giving everything else up.

Although he played with Evander whenever he came to Virginia's, he grew angry if Waylene was there as well. He considered Waylene to be evidence of Virginia's infidelity before she met him; and clearly pointed to the possibility of current and future infidelity. The existence of Waylene therefore provoked his jealousy; he suspected Virginia of making assignation after assignation. Where she was concerned, no human contact was innocent: the only possible guarantee of her fidelity was complete isolation. He cut her telephone wire, and regularly checked whom she phoned on her mobile. Any unexplained number was turned into a *casus belli*, a justification for punching her or dragging her across the room. If she dressed well he called her a slut; if she let herself go he dragged her to the glass and forced her to contemplate her slovenliness while he jeered at her.

Sometimes he would send her out to the nearest shop to bring him something he said he needed, and tell her that he expected her back in ten minutes. As soon as she had gone, he would put his watch forward to make sure that she returned late: and lateness was another *casus belli*, so he would beat her with a rising tide of indignation against her. The more he hit her, the angrier he grew.

In between times, however, and immediately afterwards, he would call her by his pet name for her, Angel, and would make prolonged love to her. He would apologise to her, become tearful, promise it would never happen again, and say that perhaps there was something wrong with him: though adding that she should try harder not to provoke him.

Irregular as his visits now were, Virginia thought about him constantly, all the time: how to please him, how not to anger or provoke him. He usually arrived very hungry and wanted a hot meal straight away. He couldn't wait, and yet everything had to be freshly prepared. Either she made him wait too long, or he didn't like what she gave him, calling it leftovers, and even hurling it at the wall in disgust. Her failure to provide him with what he wanted was further evidence of her infidelity: being too busy elsewhere, she didn't have the time to give him what he wanted.

Virginia confided in her mother a couple of times, but the first time her mother replied that she had told Virginia from the very beginning that Dwayne was no good but that she hadn't wanted to listen, and the second time that she had made her bed and now had to lie on it.

Whatever Virginia did, Dwayne was not to be propitiated. Everything was evidence of her guilt in his eyes. Sometimes he passed her in the street in his car, without letting her see him, and demanded afterwards to know where she had been, what for, and to whom she had spoken. It was as though he already knew everything, and Virginia began to feel that she was being followed and spied upon all the time. If someone smiled or laughed in the street, she assumed it was at her. She imagined that everyone around her was watching her and reporting to Dwayne: though, as she told herself, she couldn't understand why, because she wasn't doing anything.

The more she tried to please Dwayne, the angrier and more bad-tempered he became.

'You're hiding something,' he said. 'Just tell me what it is, and then we can start again.'

'There ain't nothing,' Virginia protested, half-wondering now if it was true.

For a short time Dwayne would be reasonable, even understanding.

'Just tell me what it is,' he said, 'and then we can forget it. It'll be just like it was at the beginning.'

When Virginia denied that there was anything to hide, however, Dwayne lost his temper completely. His eyes stared and became glassy, as if they had lost the power of sight; his movements became stilted, as if no longer fully under his control, but rather a manifestation of a clockwork mechanism; his speech became an emphatic monotone. When he was like this, he began to strangle her.

Her head would swim, she would start to feel faint; then, at the last minute, he would stop.

'I'm sorry, Angel,' he would say, coming to himself. 'But this time you pushed me too far.'

Then he would either dash out to get some flowers or suggest they had dinner by candlelight at a restaurant. When Virginia said that they couldn't leave Evander on his own, Dwayne pointed out that he was fast asleep and he never woke in the night. It would only be for a short time, comparatively speaking, and no harm would be done; and so Virginia agreed, in case he started to think that she had made another assignation for the night.

Virginia was sometimes tempted to take Dwayne's offer seriously, and make a new start by confessing. But what could she confess to? She couldn't think of anything. It was ages since she had socialised with anyone other than Dwayne, and he would hardly be satisfied with a confession that she had said 'Good morning' to Mr Patel who ran the local shop.

Perhaps she should confess that she had found Big Nigga, the rap star, attractive when she saw him on the television. But that was some time ago, before Dwayne smashed the screen because, he said, she was taking too much visual interest in the young hero of a soap opera. In the end, she decided not to confess because there was nothing that would have satisfied Dwayne; he was not the kind of man to be fobbed off.

The happy moments between them were fewer and fewer. But where, or to whom, could Virginia turn? Although she had always despised it, she tried the church: the First Holy Apostolic Pentecostal Church of Christ, Redeemer, a large conical brick structure with an aluminium crown of thorns at its apex, whose pastor was the founder-bishop, the Most Reverend Clyde Divine (whether that was his real name, no one knew). During the services, members of the congregation, mostly middle-aged or elderly women, stood up suddenly, crying Hallelujah! or Praise be! and starting to talk loud gibberish, some about smiting the Gideonites, until everyone joined in and the roof was raised.

At first Virginia was inclined to laugh at so many old ladies like her mother, all in broad-brimmed hats and gloves, sobbing with emotion; but then, strangely enough, she began to feel the emotion herself, weakly at first and then coming like a warm flood through her whole mind and body. Yes, Jesus was her saviour and he loved her. She knew it now. She had let Jesus into her heart.

After the service was over, and everyone had returned to normal, the Most Reverend Divine, an avuncular man of about fifty whose head was sprinkled with white curls, came to speak to Virginia. He picked her out for his attention because he had never seen her in the church before.

'Welcome, sister, welcome,' he said. 'It's your first time in the House of the Lord, isn't it?'

'Yes,' she said.

'Praise the Lord,' he said.

He was so kind, with a kindness so practised that it seemed

spontaneous, that she wanted to confide in him at once. Her chance came when he invited her to the church's Bible study meetings on Thursday evenings.

'I can't,' said Virginia.

'Why not?' asked the Most Reverend Divine. 'What could be more important than studying the Lord's word?'

Virginia told him about Dwayne. Irregular as he was in his visits, Thursday was the night he most commonly came, and there would be hell to pay if she were not there to look after him. She burst into tears: she didn't know what to do and was at her wit's end.

The Most Reverend Divine knew just what to do. He told Virginia to get down on her knees with him and pray. If she allowed God into her heart and kept Him there, he would surely answer her and tell her what to do. So they prayed together, the Most Reverend Divine imploring Almighty God to show this, his humble sinning repentant servant Virginia McStephen, how to rid herself of this unrighteous man in thrall to Satan.

The Most Reverend Divine was right: God did tell Virginia what to do. She went home with a light heart and a clear head.

Next Thursday evening, Virginia prepared for Dwayne's arrival. She filled two very large saucepans with water and put them on to boil. She also took two large frying pans and filled them with oil preparatory to heating. Someone observing her thought she might have been preparing for a large number of guests.

Then she took up a position behind the front door and waited. Great purpose is patient and she was patient; eventually her patience had its reward. She heard a scratching at the lock in the front door. It continued for a little while, like a mouse at a skirting board, as Dwayne's key searched for the keyhole. He was probably a little uncoordinated because of the cannabis and cocaine. He wasn't what you would call a heavy user, at least by comparison with his friends, but he seldom went without: he took enough to demonstrate that he was not a coward or a passive cog in the system. He, like everyone else, was his own man.

After a brief struggle, Dwayne found the keyhole and turned

the key to enter. He stepped in, the whites of his eyes inflamed with drugs and incipient anger. He was in a belligerent mood and was looking for a justification for pleasurable rage.

Virginia sprang out from behind the door. In her right hand she held a long sharp knife. Her mind was clear and, with heroic concentration and determination she recalled what she had once heard, that an upward thrust of a knife was far more dangerous than a downward one, and she let this be her guide. The Lord was with her because she got it right: the knife went in, right under the ribs, as smoothly as if she had practised a hundred times. It couldn't have been better.

Dwayne, normally so quick to anger, managed only a mild inquiry.

'What the…?'

Then he uttered a strangled, gurgling sound, fortunately not loud enough to arouse the neighbours. He slid to the ground. Its work done, Virginia cast the knife aside. It slithered down the linoleum on the hallway floor, spraying drops of blood and leaving a smear that the forensic scientists would later enjoy interpreting.

But Virginia did not rest on her laurels. She put into action the second part of the Lord's plan for Dwayne. She went to the stove and set the heat under the oil. She knew it would heat very quickly. In the meantime, she took the saucepans of boiling water and poured them over Dwayne, who was lying still in the hallway, breathing fast but very shallow. He moved a little under the torrent of scalding water, but not to any purpose, and let out a faint groan. He took no evasive action at all when she poured the spitting fat over him.

The Lord's plan had worked perfectly. A few minutes later, having taken a brief rest on her sofa, Virginia went out of her flat's front door and, in the entrance to the whole block, began to sing and dance. Her song was tuneless and her dance was nothing but a jig.

'Hallelujah! Praise be! I am the angel of the Lord.'

She repeated it over and over again. Her voice rang out through the buildings and some of the windows trembled. To begin with no one took any notice; screams were not unusual in the building. But when it continued, someone stuck his head out of his front door and shouted 'Shut up, you bitch!' When this had no effect, he shouted it again and then threatened to smash her head in if she didn't shut up. But then a group of people from the other flats began to gather round her and one of them went to her flat, whose door was open, and found the dead Dwayne. She screamed, and came out of the flat with her hand over her mouth, unable to speak further. Then she began to sob.

Virginia was still performing her jig.

'Hallelujah! Praise be! I am the Angel of the Lord!'

In custody, Virginia continued to sing and dance, as one incapable of her own distress. At first the policemen in the station were amused, but the holding cells acted as an echo chamber, and a little madness goes a long way.

The police surgeon said that she was mad and ought to go to hospital, but the hospital said that she was too dangerous for them to handle, and so the magistrate had no alternative but to remand to prison the singing and dancing defendant in the dock.

She was sent at once to the prison hospital. Doctors came to see her, both for the prosecution and the defence, but she made no distinction between them. She answered all their questions irrelevantly, incoherently and distractedly, listening for inspiration from the air and suddenly getting up from her chair and singing and dancing in a state of religious exaltation. It was difficult at times to make out what she was saying, but her refrain was clear:

'Hallelujah! Praise be! I am the Angel of the Lord!'

She ate little and slept less. She had to be kept separate from the other prisoners whose sleep she had disturbed with her nocturnal chanting, and who would have cured her insomnia with a good beating. Their threats, snarled through their cell doors at night, had no effect on her. They banged on their pipes and stamped on the floor: but still Virginia kept it up.

When she was taken to court, Virginia hardly seemed to notice the change in her surroundings. The ceremonial passed her by: the judge in his wig and red robes tried at first to be polite and reasonable with her, but soon grew irritated by the restless noisy figure in the dock. He ordered her to be taken away and tried in her absence: her lawyer having pleaded not guilty on her behalf. The facts of the case were not in dispute, nor was her madness: the judge ordered her to be detained in hospital until it was safe to release her.

The hospital was full of locked doors and barred windows, which was why it was called secure. Most of the patients were young men who had killed someone while mad, drunk or under the influence of cannabis, or all three. They each had their own room in which they played their agitating music at maximum volume to drown out that of all their peers, or as if they had all gone deaf. Occasionally a fight would break out between them for no obvious or discoverable reason, when one of them would overturn a table or a chair with a crash, and try to use the furniture as a weapon. Usually the nurses, dressed almost indistinguishably from the patients, would intervene before other than minor injuries could be inflicted.

Mostly, though, a tense calm reigned. The medicines the patients had to take made them stiff, and as unblinking as zombies. They seemed to be in a state of suspended animation, halfway between activity and inertia, and if they spoke it was in a monotone. When they watched television in the day room, whose screen flickered as eternally as the flame in the tomb of an unknown soldier, it was without interest, though their eyes flickered slightly if there was a scene of violence.

Virginia didn't like the hospital. She didn't like the young men, and the few women were even worse. Mostly they had killed their babies or set fire to where they were living, with or without fatal results. They could hardly speak two words without swearing, and their voices, being less monotonous than the men's, were full of rage. They had funny haircuts and rings through their noses. You had to be careful that your eye did not meet theirs. They called that blazing or eyeballing.

A very strange thing happened to Virginia immediately on her arrival in hospital: she stopped singing and dancing altogether. She claimed no longer to be the Angel of the Lord. The staff of the hospital found it difficult to believe that she had really changed, waiting for her to relapse and suspecting that her calm was a ruse or a deception. They attributed the change to shrewdness, an instinctive understanding that she would never get out if she expressed what was really on her mind. The door to her room had a judas-window, and sometimes she would notice that an eye from outside was applied to it. When she was in the shower, a nurse would manufacture a reason to enter and ask her a question of a kind to which she already knew the answer, so that she was patently spying on her. But there was nothing to observe, and the nurse always felt cheated of her prey.

Over and over again she was asked the same strange questions: whether she thought anyone was against her, whether, when she was on her own, anyone was talking to her, whether she had a special mission from God. However many times she answered no, they didn't seem to believe her. Once she overheard two nurses talking about her, and one of them said that she had what she called insight, that was to say she was being crafty and not revealing what she really heard and thought.

But Virginia remained patient, always did what she was told, was polite and avoided altercations, and so in the end the staff had reluctantly to admit that there was nothing wrong with her. There was nothing for it, therefore, but to start the long process of release.

At first she was accompanied on short walks in the hospital grounds by a nurse on either side of her, as if she had lost the power to walk unaided; before long, she was accompanied by only one nurse. The great day came when she was allowed out in the grounds on her own, and then for longer and longer periods. Finally, she was allowed out of the hospital altogether, first with two nurses, then with one, and lastly with none. All went well, and she was sent out for a whole weekend, on condition that she returned at the specified time – which she did.

After she had spent entire weeks at a time at home, without the faintest sign of the return of her madness, everyone was forced to agree that, there being no reason any longer to keep her, she should be released.

Virginia returned home. It was as if the burden of age and care had been lifted from her. She was young and free again. Her parents were now the legal guardians of Waylene and Evander, and looked after them full time.

Virginia went into her small kitchen to make a cup of tea. She looked around her with contentment. Before leaving the hospital, she had mentioned to the social worker that her cooker, fridge and washing machine were old and unreliable and needed replacing. The social worker had obtained a grant to do so, and they were installed just before Virginia's release.

On Friday evening, Virginia put on her best clothes and went down to the Insomnia night club, her favourite. Behind her in the queue to get in was a man a few years older than she, with a heavy gold chain round his neck and a winning smile that revealed a gold front tooth with an inlaid diamond.

- 4 -
Social Housing

THE TOWER BLOCKS rose at intervals from the ground, creating wind tunnels between them. Most of the land around had been concreted over; the grass in the few remaining patches was a scrubby brown-grey-greenish colour, scattered with plastic bottles, constantly swirling pages of tabloid newspapers, and packaging of half-eaten takeaway meals. Metal notices, now rusting, were planted at intervals in the ground:

DO NOT WALK ON THE GRASS
IT IS AN AMENITY TO BE ENJOYED BY EVERYONE
and:
NO BALL GAMES

Somewhere between Jane Austen House and Charles Dickens Tower, however, was an incongruous row of little terraced houses, of dirty bluish brick, each with a tiny back garden. It was this kind of house that the tower blocks had replaced. All of the houses, save one, were abandoned and boarded up with grey metallic sheets. The only still-occupied house was where Mrs Hardcastle lived.

Mrs Hardcastle was Mr Hardcastle's widow. She never thought of him, much less addressed him when he was alive, as anything other than Mr Hardcastle. He had been a good solid worker who drank once a week but was cheerful in drink; he put on a tie before going down to the pub; he in turn never called her other than as Mrs Hardcastle.

Unfortunately, there had been no children. This was not their wish, but there was nothing to be done about it. They had to find another source of content.

Mr Hardcastle had kept, bred and raced pigeons, until the doctor told him that it was bad for his chest, which had always been his weak point. It seemed as if his chest was where all his illnesses, when he had any, met and congregated; but, strangely enough, his chest grew no stronger when he gave his pigeons away. Perhaps it was too late, the damage had been done. But once he had given the birds away, he lost interest in life, and illnesses attacked him remorselessly. He died of what the doctor called double pneumonia, which Mrs Hardcastle took to be twice as bad as the normal kind.

His death hit her hard, of course; you don't live with a good man for fifty-four years without feeling an inconsolable grief at his departure. But no one would have known it to look at her; she had cried, but not in public because, she said, 'It wouldn't be right.'

One by one, the other residents of Sebastopol Villas – for such was the row of workmen's dwellings, erected in the 1880s, was called before the terracotta plaque fell off – had either died or been lured away by the promise of a modern flat with every convenience, such as central heating and indoor lavatories.

Mrs Hardcastle ignored the letters (she wasn't a great reader) that came offering her the same advantages, a new and better place to live, if she would agree to move out; and she thanked the man who came one day to her house to explain to her why it was uninhabitable for a number of reasons, chief among which was the outdoor water closet that must have been freezing in winter. But she said she was perfectly happy where she was, she had lived there all her married life, and hardly noticed the difficulties with which the man seemed obsessed.

Small as her garden was, she loved it and tended it with care. True, a lot of people these days seemed to throw rubbish into it, but she removed it as soon as it arrived. All things considered, she would rather stay where she was, thank you.

In fact, her garden was the only one that had not returned to urban scrub of tough, ugly plants, growing knee-high and concealing broken headless dolls, rusting bicycle wheels and broken electrical appliances.

Mrs Hardcastle's garden was neat and well-kept, a small lozenge of grass surrounded on three sides by narrow flower- beds in which there were some rose bushes and the pride of her life, a pear tree.

A flourishing tree – let alone a pear-tree – was an astonishing thing in this landscape. It is true that saplings had sometimes been planted in it by the council, but they always failed to take, either because of vandalism or some other cause, and they never grew beyond the spindly skeletal stage. The pear-tree, by contrast, burst into glorious blossom every spring, a joy that somehow dissolved the ugliness of the surroundings. Mrs Hardcastle's tree was unique.

She looked after it as though it were a child, encouraging it with words of endearment as she watered it, and cleared the weeds from around it. Perhaps this attention wasn't really necessary, but Mrs Hardcastle liked to think that it was and that without it the tree would decline and die.

The tree bore fruit as well as blossom. No doubt the strictest judges would not have awarded prizes for the pears, but in such a place a home-grown fruit was by that very fact a marvel. The local children thought that food came in multicoloured plastic wrapping, and milk in cartons. The idea of the growth or cultivation of food was alien to them; Mrs Hardcastle's tree came as a revelation to them.

Accustomed as many of them were to taking what they wanted, whether from the refrigerator at home of the nearby shops, they often stole the pears from Mrs Hardcastle's tree, but she didn't mind: they're only kids, she told herself. When she caught them at it, she ticked them off and told them that she would have given them the pears anyway if they had asked; but licit fruit never tastes as good as illicit, and only some of them thenceforth asked her permission.

One year there was a severe drought. The rains did not come to the normally damp land. The earth dried, the leaves began to shrivel, her lawn lost its greenish hue. The radio said that there had never been anything like it, at least not for twenty years or more. The levels in the reservoirs dropped, and the government ordered that no one should use more than half an inch of water for a bath. The watering of gardens was forbidden.

Mrs Hardcastle, who heard this on the radio, was very worried about her tree. How would it fare without her care and attention? It was used to as much water as it wanted. And how much the children would miss if it died! Mrs Hardcastle decided that she would continue to water the tree, but only with water that she had already used and would otherwise have thrown away.

Several times a day, then, she went out to the tree with a small bowl of water, or the saucepan in which she had boiled an egg or some potatoes, and pour it carefully at the base of the tree. While she was at it, she thought, she might as well water the roses too. After all, no one was the loser by it.

A few days later, as she poured some potato-water into the ground round the pear tree, she was startled to hear the impudent voice of a child say, 'Look what 'ardcastle's doing now!' She stood up straight, as quickly as her arthritis permitted, and looked around for the child. His voice had been unpleasantly mocking in tone, and furthermore Mrs Hardcastle didn't like the rude way in which he had called her Hardcastle. Children these days had no respect, and if she caught him she would give him what for.

She couldn't see where the little tyke had hidden himself, however. Probably he had run away. But all the same she said out loud 'I know where you are,' and that she would tell his mother. Then, with all the dignity she could muster, she returned to the house.

The little tyke was waiting for her when she went out next day to water the tree. As she poured the water, he said, 'Look, she's at it again,' and then laughed in a nasty, derisive fashion.

Surely he had something better to do than to wait for her and insult her like this?

'Now look 'ere,' said Mrs Hardcastle, but she couldn't think of anything else to say. She fled indoors: children these days could turn nasty when you crossed them.

From then on the boy, who seemed to have secreted himself very cleverly behind Mrs Hardcastle so that she was never able to catch a glimpse of him, mocked her each time she went into the garden, even before she had watered anything. 'Here she comes again,' he would say. 'She hasn't learnt nothing.'

Who was the boy talking to? Presumably he was the leader of some kind of gang. If that was so, you'd think (Mrs Hardcastle thought) you would catch sight of at least some of them as they ran away. But try as she might – she looked everywhere for them – she never did. They were just too quick for her.

Well, she'd lived through the war and had seen the bombs fall; she wasn't going to let a few kids get the better of her. She would show them what she was made of.

So she continued to go out into the garden, expecting that sooner or later the gang would tire of its silly game, tormenting an old woman like that. Instead of this, however, the leader became cheekier and more insulting as time went by. If you asked her, it was because no one brought the strap to children nowadays, as they had when she was a girl, so that they thought that they could get away with anything. And they were right – they did get away with everything.

''ardcastle's at it again,' the leader would say, or ''ardcastle's breaking the law, she'll go to prison like she deserves.' She shouted back that she'd already used the water, it was no use to anyone now, so it wasn't really watering the garden at all, not in the sense the government meant, but the boy only sneered at her. 'What's she saying now, the old biddy?'

The more Mrs Hardcastle tried to ignore the leader of the gang, the bolder he grew. Now he began to follow her into the house. 'Look,' he said, ''ardcastle's going back inside because she knows she's not supposed to be doing what she's doing. Good riddance!'

When she put the kettle on for a cup of tea, he said, "arcastle's making herself a cup of tea.' He made it sound as if it were a crime. 'She's only doing it to have some water left over.'

The rudeness of the boy distressed Mrs Hardcastle all the more because she had always given boys pears when they wanted them. Surely one of the gang, better brought up than the rest, would tell him to shut up and be a little more respectful? Instead of which, a couple of weeks after the mockery began, the boy said, as she went out to water the pear tree, 'Shall we call the coppers now?'

The final straw came when she went into the garden without any water, just to have a look, and the boy's voice, clearer than ever, said:

'Buzz off, 'ardcastle, and take yer effing roses with yer.'

Mrs Hardcastle uttered a little scream, rushed back into the house and out of the front door. She hobbled along the street – Inkerman Road – as fast as she could, and several other streets, until she came to a more frequented thoroughfare. But the boy followed her, and the gang as well, because she could hear several of them laughing at her. The leader said, 'Look at 'ardcastle, she's a real sight, she is.'

Mrs Hardcastle was a sight. She had begun to neglect herself in the last few days, her old flowered apron tied round her waist was now none too clean, and her hair was unkempt. No one took any notice of her, though, because they were used to strange sights round here, where even young people responded to invisible persecutors, where violent quarrels broke out over nothing, and shopkeepers chased shoplifters who slalomed through the crowds.

"ardcastle's on the run,' said the leader. 'Let's get after her.' And there was more derisive laughter.

Mrs Hardcastle was out of breath, and though sheer fright had loosened her joints for a time, her arthritic pains now slowed her down. Then she had a stroke of luck: she saw a policeman coming towards her. She went up to him.

'Them boys,' she said, between gasps for breath. 'It's a disgrace. I never done them no 'arm.'

The policeman looked puzzled.

'What boys?' he asked.

'Them what's shouting at me all the time and following me everywhere. They've got no respect even though I used to give them pears whenever they asked. You'd think they'd be grateful.'

'Where are these boys?' asked the policeman.

'They're be'ind me. They 'ide be'ind the fence when I come out into my garden. They're following me now.'

'Can you point them out?'

Mrs Hardcastle looked behind her, and then all round her. There were no children to be seen, only adults going about their self-absorbed business.

'They must've run away,' said Mrs Hardcastle. 'They must've dodged into the shops, they're crafty beggars. They're too quick for me.'

The policeman understood.

'How long've they been following you?' he asked.

'They been at it for over two weeks,' said Mrs Hardcastle. 'A joke's a joke. You'd've thought they'd 'ad enough of it by now.'

'I can't see them either,' said the policeman.

Mrs Hardcastle stood stock still for a moment and put her hand to her ear, as if catching something in the distance.

'There,' she said to the policeman, 'didn't you 'ear that?'

'No, what?'

'Didn't you 'ear them say, ''arcastle's shopping us to the rozzers, let's scarper.'

'Don't worry,' said the policeman. 'I'll protect you from them. You come with me, you'll be all right.'

'Aren't you going to do nothing about them. It oughtn't to be allowed, it oughtn't. They're only young, too.'

'The first thing is to make sure you're somewhere safe. We'll send someone out afterwards to catch them.'

This didn't seem a good idea to Mrs Hardcastle because they might have got far away by then. But she said nothing and the policeman radioed for a car. He whispered that one of the people who came out to fetch ought to be a woman, to reassure her.

The hospital was a large Victorian building with a Gothic tower in the middle. The police helped her up the steps to the entrance hall. Inside was a counter at which sat a man in a tie and a v-necked jumper. He was the telephonist as well as the receptionist, and was always engaged upon at least two conversations at once.

'Hello, petal,' he said to Mrs Hardcastle, and then 'Dr Brown's on annual leave,' into his mouthpiece. 'I'll call the duty doctor,' he said to the police on either side of Mrs Hardcastle, and then, 'Putting you through' to a telephonic interlocutor.

Mrs Hardcastle waited on a bench with orange imitation leather upholstery pockmarked with cigarette burns. The policeman and policewoman who had brought her stood around, chatting about the love affair of a colleague at the station. Apparently it was not going well, and they derived some pleasure from this. At least it gave them something to talk about during their fallow periods.

The duty doctor arrived, the policewoman had a word with him just out of Mrs Hardcastle's hearing, and then the police left. The doctor approached Mrs Hardcastle.

Having established that she believed she was being pursued by the boys of her neighbourhood, the young doctor, who had not shaved that morning, asked Mrs Hardcastle strange questions, such as whether she knew who the Prime Minister was, or whether she knew what a hundred less seven was. Having satisfied himself on these points (Mrs Hardcastle took no interest in politics), the doctor suggested that she stayed in hospital for a few days, 'just for a rest.' She must be tired out, he said.

She soon became a favourite on the ward, almost a pet. A few tablets taken every day were sufficient to dispel her fears: and she was very relieved that the impertinent little boy had stopped commenting on her every action, and the others had stopped laughing at her. She began to take care of herself again – she had always been a neat and tidy person, indeed had taken pride in it. She joined in willingly all the activities that the nurses said were good for her. This was in contrast to most of the other patients, who preferred to sleep all day and resented it if they were roused.

Mrs Hardcastle was sitting in the dayroom of the ward one day, in which a television was advising viewers about how they might dispel their cellulite, when a woman in her forties approached her and asked whether she might sit next to her.

'Are you Mrs Hardcastle?' she asked.

'Yes, that's right,' said Mrs Hardcastle.

'Can I call you Ivy?'

Mrs Hardcastle must have agreed, because she didn't say anything.

'Well Ivy, I'm Ms Smith, the social worker for older adults.'

'Older adults?' said Mrs Hardcastle.

'You probably call them old age pensioners,' she said with a slight laugh. 'We call them older adults because it sounds more hopeful and optimistic, less negative and stereotyped.'

Despite having made what the doctor called a full recovery, Mrs Hardcastle looked puzzled, even bemused.

'Yes,' said Ms Smith, 'these days, old age isn't what it used to be. It's all about empowering the elderly. That's why I'm here. We've got to do a bit of discharge planning and establish a suitable package of care.'

Mrs Hardcastle, it was clear, was not fully up to date.

'You see,' said Ms Smith, 'when old people have been in hospital for a little while, we can't send them home just like that.'

'Why not?' asked Mrs Hardcastle.

'All sorts of reasons,' said Ms Smith. 'For example – I'm just giving you an example, I'm not saying this will happen to you – they can go off their legs. Obviously, they can't manage at home straight away if they've been off their legs.'

'So they can't go home?'

'It's not as simple as that. They have to go home in stages, as it were. They don't need to be in hospital any more, but they're not quite ready to go home either. But anyway, we're here to talk about you.'

'When am I going home?'

'As soon as possible, of course. We don't want to keep you here longer than necessary. Apart from anything else, we need the bed.'

'When will that be?'

'As soon as we can find somewhere for you to go.'

'I can go home.'

'To Sebastapol Villas?'

'Of course, that's where I live. Where else?'

'Are you quite sure Sebastapol Villas are right for you?'

'I've lived there all me life,' said Mrs Hardcastle.

'I mean, they're very old-fashioned. There's no indoor toilet. There's no central heating. They're just not up to standard these days. I don't know how you've managed all these years.'

'It's my home,' said Mrs Hardcastle.

'I know,' said Ms Smith. 'But it's time for something better. Something more comfy. You can't go on living like that, not at your age.'

'I'm used to it,' said Mrs Hardcastle. 'And there's me gardin. I can't do without me gardin.'

'You could go to a place where there's a garden that's looked after for you. You wouldn't have to look after it yourself. That would be a treat for you, wouldn't it?'

'I love me gardening,' said Mrs Hardcastle.

'But you're too old for it now,' said Ms Smith. 'You could fall over – break your hip or something – and there'd be no one to help you. Until it was too late, of course.'

'I'll be all right,' said Mrs Hardcastle.

'That's what everyone says until it happens to them,' said Ms Smith. 'It's time to move on, Ivy. We'd all like to continue just as we've always lived, but circumstances change – we get older, for example – and we have to change with them. Sometimes it just isn't possible to go on as before.'

Mrs Hardcastle said nothing. Just then, the hearing aid of another patient, who had been inconspicuously dozing in the corner of the dayroom, began to emit a high-pitched whistle.

'I wish she'd switch that thing off,' said Ms Smith. Mrs Hardcastle, however, couldn't hear it.

It continued. Ms Smith had no choice but to go over to the old woman and ask her to turn it off. Unfortunately, she was deaf and Ms Smith had to shout at the top of her voice. When she returned to Mrs Hardcastle she appeared exhausted, and almost slumped down in the chair beside her.

'As I was saying,' she said, 'I think it's time for you to move on. You can't go on living at Sebastopol Villas.'

Mrs Hardcastle repeated that she would like to go home, and Ms Smith tried another tack.

'Put yourself in my shoes,' she said. 'Suppose you were sent home from the hospital and something happened to you. You fell and broke your hip in the garden, for example, or froze in the outdoor toilet. How do you think I would feel then? To say nothing of the official enquiry afterwards.'

Mrs Hardcastle didn't know what to say.

'You hadn't thought of that, had you?' said Ms Smith. It was a mistake to think that self-obsession was a characteristic only of youth. The old were capable of it too, not seeing things from other people's perspective.

'Wouldn't you like me to show you places where you could go instead? Places where there'd be someone on call to help you twenty-four hours a day? Some of them are very nice.'

Mrs Hardcastle evinced no enthusiasm and no opposition either.

'Right, then,' said Ms Smith, patting Mrs Hardcastle on the knee. 'I'll take you to see some tomorrow.'

True to her word, she returned to the ward the following day.

'First I'll take you to Fallowfields,' she said.

'What's that?' asked Mrs Hardcastle.

'Sheltered accommodation. You'll love it once you see it.'

Ms Smith took Mrs Hardcastle in her car and drove for about half an hour. Mrs Hardcastle was one of the few people left who had never ridden much in cars, and had to be shown the use of the seat-belt. She stared straight ahead, as if expecting disaster.

Fallowfields was a collection of small bungalows at the end of a cul-de-sac. Each had a patch of grass in front of it, but no fence between, as there had been between the back gardens of Sebastopol Villas. There were also a few dead-looking rose-bushes.

'Let's go and see the warden,' said Ms Smith brightly.

In the middle of the bungalows was an office, a kind of brick hut. A black plastic plaque, with the word MANAGER on it, was fixed to the door.

Ms Smith knocked.

'Come in,' the manager shouted, as if deafness was normal.

They entered. The manager, an Irishwoman in her fifties, asked them to sit down. She had an open and pleasing manner.

'Welcome to Fallowfields,' she said.

She brought a cup of tea for them from a kitchenette the size of a cupboard, and explained how things ran at Fallowfields.

Every resident had her own home, with kitchen and bathroom, but there was a communal hall where everyone could meet if he or she wanted to (but there was nothing compulsory). There was a pull cord in every room to raise the alarm in case of emergency, and there was someone present to answer twenty-four hours a day.

'In case you have a fall,' said Ms Smith, who clearly thought that Mrs Hardcastle was, or was soon to become, unsteady on her feet.

'There's a doctor who visits every week,' said the manager, 'and a chiropodist.'

'What's that?' said Mrs Hardcastle.

'Someone to look after your feet,' said Ms Smith.

'Feet are the weak point of quite a lot of our residents,' said the manager.

'Their Achilles heel, in fact,' said Ms Smith, and laughed.

'Do you want to see one of the bungalows?' asked the manager.

'What for?' asked Mrs Hardcastle.

'Just to see whether you like it,' said Ms Smith.

Luckily a Mrs Jones was away for a few days and had given permission for her bungalow to be shown to visitors.

They entered and were immediately enveloped in a stagnant warmth.

'Isn't it lovely and warm?' said Ms Smith to Mrs Hardcastle. 'Not at all like Sebastopol Villas.'

Indeed, the cold of Sebastopol Villas sometimes seemed not just the absence of warmth, but something positive, that emanated from the walls. Surely anyone would want to live somewhere warmer.

Mrs Jones had a collection of china horses – hundreds and hundreds of them. She also had vases with bright red and blue plastic flowers. In the sitting room was a large television.

'It's very cosy, isn't it?' said Ms Smith enthusiastically. 'I could live here myself.'

The visit over, Ms Smith drove Mrs Hardcastle back to the hospital.

'It was lovely, wasn't it?' said Ms Smith. 'You'd be much better off there – or somewhere like it – don't you think?'

Actually, Mrs Hardcastle couldn't go to Fallowfields, because it was full and there was a long waiting list to get in. She would have to go to somewhere like Senior Court, a much larger establishment, where the silence of the deathbed was punctuated only by the screams of the demented. The staff there spent most of their day locked in the office, drinking coffee and chain-smoking. But at least it was warm, better than Sebastopol Villas.

'No, I'd like to go home,' said Mrs Hardcastle.

Whenever old people were particularly obstinate, Ms Smith adopted a very sweet tone, in which reason and compassion fought for the upper hand.

'You don't have to decide now,' she said. 'You can think about it.'

Mrs Hardcastle didn't think about it, nor did she have to, because she already knew what she wanted. She wanted to go home.

Ms Smith visited her two or three times a week to find out if she had given any thought to Fallowfields, and had changed her mind. Every time she came, she used the same arguments: Sebastopol Villas were cold and damp, she was isolated and vulnerable there, Fallowfields was warm and there would be company for her there. But Mrs Hardcastle still wanted to go home.

The matter became urgent, however. Ms Smith came one day and sat next to her instead of bending over her, as she had done on her previous visits.

'The service is being reconfigured,' she said to Mrs Hardcastle.

Mrs Hardcastle showed no sign of having understood.

'The service is being reconfigured,' repeated Ms Smith. 'That means this ward is closing. You'll have to go somewhere else.'

'So I can go home?' said Mrs Hardcastle.

'Well not exactly,' said Ms Smith. 'The services are being reconfigured to make them more efficient. We have to consider best practice and value for money. And it's been decided that this ward represents neither, so it's closing in a week's time. A new Chief Executive's been appointed, and you know how a new broom sweeps clean.'

Old age being a time of reduced horizons, Mrs Hardcastle did not appear to take much interest in what Ms Smith said.

'That means we'll have to think of somewhere for you to go,' said Ms Smith. 'And quickly.'

'I'd like to go home.'

There was nothing for it, then: Ms Smith had hoped to avoid having to take this step, but now she saw that it was unavoidable.

'You'll have to come with me, Ivy. I'll have to show you.'

She took Mrs Hardcastle once more in her car, but this time to Sebastopol Villas – or to what had until recently been Sebastopol Villas. It was now a pile of rubble, having been demolished.

'There was a compulsory purchase order on Sebastopol Villas because they were unfit for human habitation. Now do you see why we have to find somewhere else for you to go?'

But Mrs Hardcastle wasn't listening to Ms Smith. She was listening to someone else.

'Buzz off, 'ardcastle, and take yer effing roses with yer.'

- 5 -
Only a Piece of Paper

MR MONTAGU, the rich widower and businessman, who was in his late middle age, had a large part of his bowel cut out because of cancer. Until the discovery of the tumour he had never had a day's illness, but he bore the indignities of hospital and surgery with fortitude, even though he was more used to giving orders than to receiving them.

He was unassuming and undemanding in the hospital, making no complaint if a meal was not to his liking, or if the surgeon came on his rounds later than expected. He was not fractious, as many in his situation were. He did not protest against fate by persecuting those who were trying to rescue him from it.

The operation was a success and his recover uneventful. Still, the operation weakened him and it was a few days before he was allowed home. During these days he displayed none of that self-important impatience that men accustomed to successful activity often show in the face of natural processes, such as healing, that are refractory to their wills. He was obviously wiser than other men of his type.

He was grateful for everything that was done for him, though in a polite and detached way. When it was time for him to leave the hospital, he bought a large box of chocolates of the best quality for the nurses, though he was unsure whether they would be able to distinguish them from less expensive varieties.

He presented them to Sister Lee, the Chinese nurse in charge of all the others. She thanked him and told him that he need not have bothered: it had been a pleasure to look after him.

He went home to his elegant flat in a quietly fashionable eighteenth-century square. By now he had come to accept his loneliness and even, when too long in the presence of others, to like it. Other people were inclined to noise and Mr Montagu prized silence, all the more so after his operation. Although he was told that, as far as the surgeon was able to discern, all his cancer had been removed, it was impossible for Mr Montagu not to feel that he had been touch by, if not definitively marked out for, death. In the circumstances, extraneous and unnecessary noise was burdensome and even – though Mr Montagu had long ceased to follow the religion of his forefathers – sacrilegious.

About two weeks after his return home, while his cleaning lady was fussing over things that were already clean (for a widower of his age and orderly habits did not generate much to do), he heard the post arrive through his letter box. There was only one letter, from the hospital, but it was not official. It was hand written.

Dear Mr Montagu (it went),

When you are in the ward I see that you are a very nice gentleman. You are very kind and smiling, even when in pain. You are also handsome.

Therefore I would like very much to meet you again, as nowadays there are not very nice gentlemen to meet. Here is my address and telephone number. Thank you for calling/writing to me.

Yours very sincerely,

Victoria Lee (Miss)
Ward sister of your ward

Mr Montagu was astonished. In fact, he had to sit down to read it a second time. Was it a declaration of love from someone from an alien land who did not know how these things were done here? Mr Montagu, though well-disposed towards her, had scarcely noticed Sister Lee. She was neither beautiful nor ugly, she was thin as Chinese working women tended to be, a presence rather than a personality, who seemed to value efficiency for its own sake rather than because it brought comfort to the patients. He would have guessed that she thought that emotion of any kind was an impediment to the smooth running of the ward. He assumed – or rather, he would have assumed if he had thought about it – that for her he was just another patient, an animated statistic at best, an interruption to routine at worst, rather than a living, breathing man. Certainly, he had done everything in his power not to stand out from the other patients, not to magnify his importance or claim that his needs or wishes should be attended to first, before those of everyone else. Now it appeared that he had succeeded so well in maintaining his modesty of demeanour that he had stood out because of it. But all the same, he had done nothing, absolutely nothing, to encourage Sister Lee to develop an affection for him, on that point his conscience was quite clear.

How, if at all, should he answer? To answer would be to encourage; but not to answer would be cold-hearted or cruel. Although time and thought would not necessarily resolve the dilemma, experience had taught Mr Montague not to rush into replies to disturbing letters. Right solutions came not by a process of rational thought, but by a process of precipitation in the mind. He would sleep on it.

The next day, having other matters to attend to, Sister Lee disappeared from his thoughts. Caring for his investments, now that he was retired and dependent upon their yield, was not only good mental exercise but essential to his well-being. By no means avaricious, and not desirous of becoming the biggest fish in whatever pool he found himself (a disease of youth from which he had long been cured), he nevertheless had the businessman's sense that unless he was becoming richer he was becoming poorer. Merely to maintain a fortune was therefore not enough.

On the following day, however, another letter from the hospital arrived. Mr Montagu knew at once that it would be from Sister Lee, and it was.

Dear Mr Montagu,

I hope you are not suffering from any complications so you cannot write. I am waiting very hopefully for your answer because you are such a polite man.

Yours very sincerely,

Victoria Lee (Miss)

Mr Montagu smiled. There was a certain naïve, bittersweet charm to the letters that disarmed him and caused a faint warmth to course through his veins. Surely only a very sad person would expose herself in this way to contumacious and humiliating rejection? Then a dark and unpleasant thought crossed his mind: suppose she were an unscrupulous gold-digger? How stupid he would look if, at his age, and with his knowledge of the world, he should fall prey to the machinations of a common schemer? One who, moreover, was not a raging beauty over whom any man might lose his head? Mr Montagu was not particularly sensitive to the opinion of others, but like most men he did not want to be a laughing stock. What would his children think?

But no, he thought again, she could not be a schemer, for she could know nothing of his circumstances. True, his treatment in the hospital had been very expensive, she must have known that, but he might merely have been well-insured through his work, like most of the patients. She would have known that he was a widower – that much would have been clear from the hospital notes – but that she chose a widower rather than a married man was really rather to her credit than otherwise.

Why not contact her? What harm could come of it and

what, really, had he to lose? If he were honest, he had accommodated himself to being alone from necessity, not from choice or taste for his own company: in other words, he had made the best of a bad situation. He had interests to absorb him, true enough: he tended his bonsai trees, for example, and read voraciously, particularly on historical subjects. He had even become a collector, in a small way, of old, elaborately engraved share certificates, particularly of the Ottoman Empire, which were a window on the past, or at least on a part of the past. But all the interests in the world did not equal one human contact, and while his business career had left him with many acquaintances, even friendly acquaintances, it had left him with few friends: for in the business world, people were friendly in proportion to their usefulness, and the fact is that Mr Montagu, now quietly living on his investments, was not useful any more. In addition, people in business were impatient of those who had been very ill and like to die, for mortal illness did not enter their calculations and, insofar as it raised disturbing questions about the real worth of their ambitions, was cast out of their minds by a mental Iron Curtain. They were not so much fully rational as very calculating, and superstitious about illness, as if all types of illness were contagious. They wanted nothing more than necessary to do with the ill, or even with the cured.

Sister Lee, of course, was different. She knew all about his condition – more than he knew himself, in fact – but it did not put her off. She had seen him at his lowest point, at his most vulnerable and unattractive, denuded of the clothes that alone can give dignity to the old. She had seen him with his unpleasant abdominal wound. She had thus looked beyond the surface to the man within; and that spoke well of her.

Besides, he had heard that eastern women were obliging to the point of subservience. Mr Montagu was by no means a dictatorial man, in search of someone to dominate, but it was undeniable that, in his present weakened condition, it might be pleasant to have someone whose main object in life was to please him. The last thing he needed was a power struggle in his own home, of the kind that too often occurred these days between men and women. He wanted above all to avoid complication.

All things considered, then, a reply to Miss Lee was perfectly in order. She might perfectly fulfil his need for companionship without emotional depth and all the undercurrents that depth brought with it. Nothing ventured, nothing gained.

Besides, any initial contact with Miss Lee was like buying something on approval. If things turned out badly, there was no commitment to continue.

Mr Montagu sat down at his desk to write. Although an articulate and sometimes even an eloquent man, the correct form of words came to him on this occasion with great difficulty. He had no experience of this kind of thing. Unusually, he found it necessary to draft version after version, striking out words that had seemed appropriate to him only moments before, when they were in his mind, but which looked foolish or stilted once committed to paper.

At length, however, he could improve it no further, and sent it as it was:

Dear Miss Lee,

Thank you for your letter. You and your staff were very kind and attentive to me when I was in hospital. I could not have wished for better care.

Your letter surprised me because I was not aware that I was any more to you than just another patient among many others.

It would be very pleasant to meet again. If it is convenient for you, please ring me on the number above, and we will arrange things.

With kind regards.
Yours sincerely.

Two days later, at about six in the evening, Mr Montagu's telephone rang.

'Can I speak to Mr Montagu, please.'

'Speaking.'

'I am Victoria Lee – Miss.'

'How are you, Miss Lee?' Mr Montagu felt at once that his question sounded odd, false even, as if she had been the patient and he the nurse.

'I am very well, thank you, Mr Montagu,' said Miss Lee.

There followed a stilted conversation during which the real subject on their minds was not mentioned. It was like being an adolescent again, Mr Montagu thought: awkward and unsure how to proceed.

They discussed Mr Montagu's scar (completely healed) and his bowel habit (once again regular after a period of turbulence), and finally agreed to meet in an Italian restaurant, neither plush nor basic, expensive nor cheap, at a time of the evening neither early nor late.

After an initial period of awkwardness, the evening went surprisingly well. After one drink, Miss Lee flushed a little and began to laugh in a bird-like, but not stupid, way. She began to call him Montagu, as if that were his first name, and he found it charming. She told him about her life in Malaya, which is where she came from; her father, until his death, had had a shop in a small town on the banks of a great brown river. Mr Montagu told her proudly of his children, his son an advertising executive, and his daughter a producer at the BBC.

She had wanted desperately to escape the muddy banks and sacks of rice among which she had grown up. How she had loved the asphalt and paving when she had first come to England to train as a nurse, that did not turn slithery in the rain! How wonderful to get away from all that bargaining, all that haggling, with its bogus protestations of inability to pay more or to accept less! Here, you just decided what you wanted and whether you could afford it; no nerve-wracking trials of will. It was possible to live quietly here, with no one knowing, or caring, who you were or what you did.

At the end of the evening, they agreed to go to the theatre together.

Miss Lee began to stay three or four nights a week in Mr Montagu's elegant flat. She did not move in completely, nor did either of them suggest that she should. She kept her own flat and Mr Montagu never went there. Nor did she ever meet his children: they were not kept out of sight of each other, but somehow their paths never crossed. It was the perfect arrangement, a permanent courtship.

They went to the theatre together, to concerts, the cinema, restaurants. Mr Montagu would buy her small things – trinkets, really, but expensive – that pleased her inordinately.

And she in turn made his flat more comfortable by little touches that reduced the impersonality of a single man's taste. Together, they had the pleasures of intimacy without its tensions: their company seemed sufficient to each other, and they never indulged in the furious quarrels that some couples indulge in to persuade themselves that there is feeling left between them.

They had been happy together for more than a year when Miss Lee received a letter that troubled her deeply. It came from Malaya and was written in Chinese. She carried it with her wherever she went, and from time to time would remove it from her bag, unfold it and sigh over it. She did this sometimes in Mr Montagu's presence.

'What's the matter?' he would ask.

'Nothing,' replied Miss Lee.

'There must be something, or you wouldn't sigh like that.'

Miss Lee would then fold the letter and put it back in her bag.

'Who's the letter from?' asked Mr Montagu.

It was only after several times of asking when, despite his habitual patience, he displayed the first signs of exasperation, that she told him that it was from her mother.

'Is she ill?' he asked solicitously.

'No,' said Miss Lee.

'Then what is it?'

'Nothing,' said Miss Lee.

Eventually, Mr Montagu told her that she must tell him what in the letter was bothering her, especially as she had now received another one.

Miss Lee saw that she had no alternative but to tell Mr Montagu, though it made her uncomfortable to do so.

'My mother would like to visit me,' she said.

Mr Montagu laughed.

'Is that all?' he said. 'Why didn't you tell me before? Of course she can come and visit you. What's the problem in that?'

Miss Lee was silent again. She looked down at the floor.

'What's the matter now, Victoria?' asked Mr Montagu.

There was a long silence, and then Miss Lee said:

'She can't afford the fare.'

In more than a year, Miss Lee had never asked Mr Montagu for anything. She received whatever he gave her with pleasure, of course, and thanked him politely for it, but she had never expressed a desire for anything, not even by so much as a movement of her eyes in the direction of something she coveted, in case he took it as a request. Mr Montagu sensed with what difficulty Miss Lee had mentioned that her mother could not afford the fare.

'I'll pay it for her,' he said.

A younger woman from a different part of the world might have squealed with delight and flung her arms round Mr Montagu's neck, and kissed him; but such was not Miss Lee's way. She did not smile; instead, she looked sad.

'It is impossible,' she said. 'She couldn't accept.'

'Why not?' said Mr Montagu.

'You are a stranger. She doesn't know you.'

'She doesn't need to know it comes from me. I could give you the money and you could buy the ticket. There's no difficulty there.'

'But it wouldn't be true, it would be a lie.'

'A white lie, and a small one at that. It's only to make her happy, after all.'

Miss Lee accepted after some hesitation, and after a few more attempts at refusal. They sent her mother a ticket to come in a month's time.

They drove to the airport together to collect her. Mr Montagu's car, which he seldom used, was a powerful one, smooth and comfortable, a cocoon of luxury in a disordered and uncomfortable world. It was the car of a man of distinction and though Miss Lee said nothing, she noticed it.

They stood together at the arrivals gate, waiting for her mother to emerge. Crowds of people came out in spurts, like water from a malfunctioning tap.

'Would you rather wait for her alone?' asked Mr Montagu.

'No, she knows all about you,' said Miss Lee.

When Miss Lee's mother emerged, it seemed as if she was swept along on a tide, like a small piece of flotsam. She was a tiny woman, dressed in black pyjamas and grey slippers, who looked as if she must have travelled by accident.

Victoria stepped forward to greet her once she had passed the barrier. It was not an emotional reunion. There was no physical contact between them and no signs of joy or even pleasure. Except for her mode of dress, her mother might just as well have arrived for a business meeting as to see her daughter.

Miss Lee presented her to Mr Montagu. She spoke not a word of English and merely lowered her eyes a little, and nodded faintly, as recognition of his existence.

Although – or was it because? – she had never left her town before, she showed no curiosity about her surroundings. Clearly she had not come to see the sights, though it was at her own instigation that she came. In the car, on the way back, she talked a little to her daughter, but though Mr Montagu spoke no Chinese, he had the impression that this was no idle chatter, no mere catching up after a long separation.

It had been agreed that, Miss Lee's flat being tiny, and Mr Montagu's flat being large, Miss Lee's mother should stay with him. This was not an arrangement that Mr Montagu had ever anticipated with much pleasure, but now he had met her he looked forward to it with foreboding. To live with someone without a word of language in common was difficult enough even when non-verbal communication was possible; but Miss Lee's mother appeared uncommunicative even with the aid of language, her face giving away nothing. The next three weeks

– the duration of her stay – were not going to be easy, to put it mildly, even though Miss Lee promised to come at every opportunity her duty rota permitted.

Miss Lee's mother established herself quickly in Mr Montagu's flat, however. Whether she appraised it in any way, whether for example she took its size and furnishings as evidence of its owner's wealth, was impossible to tell. To all appearances, she took everything for granted, as if she had lived all her life in such a flat. She was surprised by nothing, and examined nothing.

She kept mainly to her own room. Victoria had warned Mr Montagu that she would eat only Chinese food and prepared everything in advance for her. She would not try so much as a slice of bread: her life in the town by the river bank had left her as undeviating from her habits as a tram, the slightest deviation representing not a detour but a disaster. And yet the first journey of her life had been one of eight thousand miles.

It was only natural, of course, that she should not venture from the flat with Mr Montagu, since he would not have been able to explain to her anything that she saw; but she evinced no desire to go out with her daughter either.

She talked a little with her daughter when she came, or rather seemed to make pronouncements to which her daughter replied by only a word or two; she seemed to take no particular pleasure in her daughter's company and Mr Montagu thought he could detect a harsh timbre in her voice, as if she were uttering unpalatable truths which it was her duty to propound. Mr Montagu did not enquire of Miss Lee what these were, just in case her mother's apparent lack of English were only a ruse to make him unwary. He began to have the uncomfortable feeling that he was being watched in his own home.

Certainly Miss Lee's mother was a brooding presence in the flat, even when – as most of the time she did – she stayed in her own room. What she did in her room was a mystery. She appeared to have brought no reading matter with her, and she never turned on the television though Victoria had showed her how. Mr Montagu was aware that the Chinese were not a religious people, so it was unlikely that she spent her time in prayer or even in meditation. Of course, how she spent her time was entirely up to her, it was her choice; but even though she was silent, at most padding around no more noisily than a cat, Mr Montagu could not rid himself of an awareness of her presence. She seemed watchful; he couldn't even leave the flat while she was there, because he couldn't explain to her where he was going and when he would be back. It would have been as irresponsible to leave her on her own as to leave a child on its own. It was as if she had imprisoned him.

During the three weeks that Miss Lee's mother stayed, Mr Montagu hardly spoke to Miss Lee; but at his age, three weeks, however ill-spent, is not an eternity, and he was soon enough driving Miss Lee and her mother back to the airport for her return flight. The mother was still wearing black pyjamas, though whether the same pair it was impossible to tell.

The parting of mother and daughter was as unemotional as their reunion had been. As he saw the tiny woman disappear into the maw of the departure hall, Mr Montagu felt a weight fall from his shoulders. So light a woman, so heavy a burden! Now life could resume its pleasant, even tenor.

As was only natural, this did not happen straight away. Her mother's presence had been a strain on Miss Lee, too; her normally unlined face had developed some wrinkled while her mother was there. On the way back from the airport, they hardly spoke; Mr Montagu could not express his feelings of relief, at least until Miss Lee had made her own feelings clear, for fear of giving offence. And since, as he knew, filial piety was so important to the Chinese, it was probable that she would never let him know what she felt.

However, two months after the departure of her mother, it was clear that Miss Lee was not returning to her normal, pre-visitation self. On the contrary, she remained tense and monosyllabic. When they went out together, she ate without appetite, looked at pictures without seeing them, and listened to music without hearing it. She seemed to enjoy nothing as she had before; in short, she was preoccupied.

'What's the matter, Victoria?' Mr Montagu asked.

'Nothing,' said Victoria with surprising vehemence. And though she was otherwise very self-controlled, Mr Montagu could tell that the muscles in her face were, despite her best efforts, tightly clenched.

He let the matter drop for now, but repeated his question in two weeks' time, receiving the same answer.

'But Victoria,' said Mr Montagu, 'there's obviously something the matter. You must tell me what it is.'

But this importunity only angered her, so that her silence was not merely the absence of words, but something positive and almost aggressive. Mr Montagu began to feel tense in her presence, for fear of breaking in on her world unbidden.

One day, Mr Montagu found Miss Lee reading a letter while she was sitting on his sofa. It was in Chinese, and he guessed who it was from. The fact that she was reading it in his presence emboldened him to ask her about it.

'It's from my mother,' Miss Lee said.

'What does it say?'

'She says you are a very nice man.'

Mr Montagu laughed, a short explosive laugh, for Miss Lee's mother had shown no sign of regard for him while she was living his flat. Miss Lee, however, did not give the impression that she thought she had said anything funny.

'I wonder how she discovered that,' said Mr Montagu. 'She couldn't have understood a word I said.'

'She says I must marry you,' said Miss Lee.

Mr Montagu smiled, but without mirth: more as a grimace. 'I don't see what she has to do with the matter,' he said.

'She said so before she left,' said Miss Lee.

'You should tell her it's none of her business.'

Miss Lee fell silent. This is not how the Chinese speak to their parents. Westerners did, perhaps, with what result was only too plain to see.

Although Mr Montagu thought that he now understood the reason for Miss Lee's change of mood, this understanding altered nothing. He tried to jolly her along, and he appealed to her rationality. After all, he asked her, what had really changed between them? They could go out together as before. The food in the restaurants was just as good, the music just as inspiring, the plays just as absorbing, as before. They were both of an age to decide for themselves how they lived, and how they had lived before the visit was perfectly agreeable to them both. There was therefore no objective need for change.

Mr Montagu was surprised, and displeased, to discover that his arguments, though perfectly sound, had no effect. Miss Lee did not so much side with her mother as appear to believe that she had to obey her. It was not that she was herself desperate to marry Mr Montagu; the question hadn't arisen before the visit; and if Mr Montagu had asked her but her mother had forbidden it, she would have refused him. But now the question obviously obsessed her, especially after she began to receive regular and frequent letters from her mother.

'Why worry so much what your mother wants?' said Mr Montagu. 'She's thousands of miles away.'

Miss Lee was silent.

'What can she do to you? Witchcraft?' Mr Montagu laughed again, but somehow his laughter sounded hollow. He decided on another tack, equally rational. 'Why is it so important to get married anyway? It's only a piece of paper.'

Miss Lee looked down at the floor and said nothing.

'We have theatre tickets,' said Mr Montagu. 'Restoration comedy. You'll love it. There's nothing like it when it's well done.'

Miss Lee went, of course; she always did what Mr Montagu suggested. But the broad, no less than the subtle, comedy of the play escaped her. She sat through it with the immobile expression of a professional mourner. It was as if there was nothing in the world, past, present or to come, to laugh at.

She continued to spend three or four nights a week in Mr Montagu's company, but appeared to derive no pleasure from it. Neither, now, did Mr Montagu; quite the reverse in fact. These complications were precisely what he had not wanted; he hated the tension of things that were unsaid. He began to curse himself for an old fool for having mixed himself up in such a situation, against which (as he now saw) anyone would have advised him had he asked. A fool and his tranquillity are soon parted.

How clear and straightforward were business affairs by comparison with affairs of the heart! You bought or you sold, and that was that; no silent reproaches, no hidden meanings, everything could be put down in black and white. Mr Montagu began to dread the arrival of Miss Lee, and would retreat to his papers in his study when she came, pleading matters that required his immediate attention to avoid her company, or her presence, which seemed to affect the room she was in like sound-proofing, deadening the slightest noise.

This can't go on, thought Mr Montagu, but he thought it for quite a long time before he did anything about it. Eventually, he plucked up the courage to say something.

'Victoria, this isn't working.'

A flicker of distress agitated Miss Lee's face for a moment, before it settled back into immobility.

'I mean, you're not getting any pleasure from my company, and therefore I feel bad too. And let's face it, the whole point is to enjoy ourselves.'

Miss Lee looked past him, hardly blinking.

'We're both too old for domestic scenes,' he added.

Miss Lee considered for a moment and then stood up. She walked to the bedroom where she had a capacious embroidered bag in which she had brought her personal things to the flat, and began to pack it. It was obvious that she was preparing to leave.

'Victoria,' said Mr Montagu, suddenly wondering whether, after all, it couldn't go on, 'can't we talk about it?'

But Miss Lee continued her round of collecting her things. When she had finished, she went to the front door, Mr Montagu following her.

'Goodbye, Mr Montagu,' she said, and left, shutting the door behind her.

Three days after Miss Lee's departure, Mr Montagu received a call from hospital – not the one in which Miss Lee worked.

'Mr Montagu?'

'Speaking.'

'You are the fiancé of Victoria Lee?'

Mr Montagu was taken aback to be so described. But he sensed that the moment was not opportune to explain the precise state of his relations with Miss Lee.

'In a manner of speaking,' he said.

'She's out of intensive care,' said the voice from the hospital.

'I didn't know...'

'She took an overdose. She's out of danger.'

Mr Montagu felt a mixture of relief and annoyance, perhaps with the latter predominating. He could foresee a prolonged period of turmoil, useless but time and energy-consuming, ahead. The prospect depressed him. He had hoped for a clean break.

'Can I tell her you will be visiting?'

'I suppose so,' he said.

He was aware that he sounded ungracious, but he had wanted to refuse. Of course, the person at the other end of the line couldn't be expected to know that his reply was a compromise between obligation and inclination.

'At what time?'

'This afternoon.'

With a reluctance that manifested itself as a dragging sensation in the pit of his now-healed stomach, Mr Montagu went to the hospital. He took some flowers and found the ward in which Miss Lee was a patient. She had a room of her own.

Their meeting was not a reconciliation. Miss Lee did not smile when he entered and though he tried to do so himself, he was aware that it must have looked more like a snarl, a baring of fangs, than a smile. For some reason the title of a best-selling book of a few years before, *What Do You Say after You've Said Hello*, ran through his mind.

Miss Lee was barely monosyllabic, and when Mr Montagu told her that it had been raining on his way to the hospital, she turned her head from him. His words sounded ridiculous, and polite conversation was now out of the question; so, however, was anything more to the point. After half an hour during which nothing had been concluded or even broached, he left with relief.

The next day he received another call from the hospital.

'Miss Lee has been transferred to the psychiatric ward.'

Mr Montagu asked why, though the answer, really, was obvious.

'She's refusing to eat. She hardly speaks. She says she wants to die and will kill herself.'

Mr Montagu went to the psychiatric ward. He met the doctor there in charge of the case who asked him whether he could throw any light on Miss Lee's state of mind. Had she ever been like this before? Mr Montagu didn't know. Did she drink a lot? A glass or two of wine at most, and then not every day. Did she gamble (the Chinese were great gamblers)? Not as far as he knew. What, then?

The doctor was considerably younger than Mr Montagu, closer to the age at which one might expect *chagrins d'amour*. Mr Montagu therefore felt embarrassed by what he had to relate, but he felt it was his duty to relate it.

'Everything went well,' he said, 'until her mother came from Malaya. For some reason she exerts an all-powerful influence on her daughter. She obviously told her that she had to marry me. Ever since then, Victoria changed. She became quiet and sullen. I couldn't get a word out of her. To be honest, I couldn't stand it anymore.'

'Before that, you were happy?'

'Yes, very. We did everything together. Then her mother came along.'

'And spoiled everything by insisting that Victoria married you?'

'Yes, I couldn't understand why. After all, it's only a piece of paper.'

The doctor paused for a moment.

'If it's only a piece of paper,' he asked, 'why don't you sign it?'

'That's absurd,' said Mr Montagu. 'You don't do things just because it doesn't matter whether you do them or not.'

The doctor said nothing, and Mr Montagu felt slightly uncomfortable, as if he had just failed an oral exam.

'I'm not giving in to blackmail,' he said.

The doctor made a non-committal sound and then told Mr Montagu that Miss Lee had announced to the staff that she would kill herself at four o'clock in the afternoon, in two days' time, unless Mr Montagu had offered to marry her by then.

'You see what I mean,' said Mr Montagu. 'It wouldn't be a good foundation for a marriage, would it?'

The doctor studiously avoided taking sides. He merely said:

'I think she means it.'

'Surely not,' said Mr Montagu. 'People who talk about it never actually do it.'

'I'm afraid that's a myth,' said the doctor. 'Most people who kill themselves have let someone know beforehand.'

'But still most people who talk about it don't do it,' said Mr Montagu. 'That's the important thing to remember.'

'Besides,' said the doctor, 'you have to remember two things. The Chinese set great store by not losing face. If they've said they're going to do something, they feel they have to do it, or they will lose face. She's told a lot of people she's going to kill herself. And the second thing you have to remember is her personality.'

'What do you mean?'

'Does she strike you as the kind of person to make idle threats? She's not an adolescent girl.'

Mr Montagu drew in a deep breath.

'I can't just give in to her,' he said, 'can I?'

The doctor didn't reply. Instead, he said:

'Of course, we'll try to look after her. Things will change in time, they always do.'

'They'll have to,' said Mr Montagu, sounding firm but feeling apprehensive. And he left the hospital.

On the day and at the time appointed, Miss Lee did try to kill herself. A nurse had been deputed to keep her within sight at all times, but she was young and inexperienced, and Miss Lee prevailed on her to allow her to go alone to the toilet. The nurse did not see how she could refuse: a necessity was a necessity, even if you were suicidal. So she let her go and waited outside.

When it dawned on her that Miss Lee was being a strangely long time, the nurse called out 'Are you all right?' to which Miss Lee replied that she was.

But shortly thereafter, at four o'clock precisely, the nurse heard a thump on the ground.

'Are you all right, Vicky?' she asked anxiously.

There was no answer, only a faint gurgling sound.

The nurse gave the door, which was of flimsy construction, a kick; but flimsy as it was, it did not open. She went to get help.

When the door was broken down (the key that was supposed to open it from the outside having been lost), Miss Lee was found slumped on the narrow strip of the floor. She had hidden a nylon stocking about her, wrapped it round her neck and pulled sharply on the two ends.

'I didn't know you could do it like that,' said a male nurse.

'Never mind that,' said the nurse in charge. 'Let's pull her out and give her mouth-to-mouth.'

Fortunately, Miss Lee, who had not been breathing when they found her, came round quite quickly. It would have been difficult to explain how and why, when it was documented so clearly that she had announced the time and day of her suicide, she had been able to carry out her threat. The enquiry would not have accepted the excuse that she asked to go to the toilet a quarter of an hour before the event: everyone would have been blamed, as if the job were an easy one.

When Miss Lee came round, she appeared surprised and disappointed at first, but then she became docile and obedient. She accused herself of foolishness and apologised to the staff for all the trouble she had caused. She said she had learned her lesson and would never do such a thing again. This enabled the staff to report to the doctor that her attempts had been only a gesture, a manifestation of her manipulative personality. They called it 'behaviour,' the opposite of illness, and a term of reproach.

At any rate, her attempted self-strangling seemed to have

acted as a catharsis on Miss Lee. She became cheerful – 'But not too cheerful,' the nurses added – and helped around the ward as if she were one of the staff rather than a patient. One of the young doctors, an enthusiast, discoursed on the effect of a shock on the chemicals in the brain that brought about this change. He made strangulation sound like therapy.

Miss Lee asked to leave the hospital, and there seemed no good reason to deny her request. Indeed, there was no reason why she should not return to work, as she said she wanted. And so she left.

The staff informed Mr Montagu by telephone of her departure; he thanked them politely, but said that she was not a relative of his.

Miss Lee returned to work, but shortly afterwards her annual holiday was due. She went on holiday.

Three months later, Mr Montagu received a telephone call from Miss Lee's hospital, from someone who called herself the Director of Nursing. Did he know anything of Miss Lee's whereabouts? She had not returned from her holiday, which was most unlike her because she was so punctilious in the performance of her duty.

Mr Montagu knew nothing. How, indeed, could he have known anything? Two months before, Miss Lee's body had been found floating in the sluggish brown river there, and deaths in Malaya are not usually notified in England.

- 6 -
Identity Crisis

WHEN THE STAFF of the Roxy-Carlton Cinema opened it for the midday showing of a film that no one wanted to see, at any rate at that time of day, they were surprised to observe a man leave the hall in a furtive, sideways fashion. He must have slept there overnight.

'Hey, you...' one of the staff shouted, but the man took no notice and slipped out of the cinema's front door into the street outside, rushing down the street and not looking back. The staff of the cinema soon forgot about him. Luckily, he had left no mess behind him that they would have felt mildly obliged to clear up

The man was about forty years old, slightly built and an inch or two below medium height, with no obvious features that would have imprinted them on anyone's memory at first glance. There was no reason for anyone to take any notice of him.

The cinema was in the middle of a busy shopping street in a fashionable-enough quarter of the vast city. When he had slowed down fully clear of the cinema, the man looked right and left to decide which way to go; but since he recognised nothing, and had no purpose to fulfil, the decision was an arbitrary one, the most difficult kind to take. How we depend upon circumstances to take our decisions for us! But the man had no circumstances to speak of and therefore his mind was blank when he considered the question. Only his desire not to be seen to be loitering, which might have drawn the attention of people to him, impelled him forward; therefore, he turned left.

He slowed his pace once he was certain that he was out of sight of the cinema staff. He had nothing to do, but the mind abhors a vacuum and so he stopped at every shop window to stare intently in, as if he had never in his life seen the kind of things displayed in them. A pharmacy with a display of a new medicated shampoo was as amazing to him as an antique shop displaying old red-lacquered Chinese furniture and a bronze mythological lion. It was as if, for him, the world was entirely new; as if he were discovering the existence of flowers in a stand outside a grocer's, and of newspapers outside a newsagent's. 'Prime Minister in Trouble:' what was a Prime Minister? It was as if he had been born able to read, but knowing absolutely nothing else.

He walked on. People passed him in the street without taking any notice of him. He recognised no one, and no one recognised him. Inside, he felt a strange emptiness; something, obviously, was missing, but he couldn't say what. Then he felt a gnawing inside and tried to put a name to it. Eventually it came to him: hunger. He felt hungry.

He put his hand in his pocket and felt around. What for? Ah yes, money, that was it, money that came in coins and notes. But his pockets were empty, not only those of his trousers but of his jacket too. Not only was there no money in them, but there was nothing else either. There was no wallet, no letter, no document that could have given him a clue as to who he was or why he was where he was. He was a man who had been cut loose from life, like an empty boat that had slipped its moorings.

He continued on his way, if a random peregrination can be called a way. Although the world was entirely new to him, he soon grew bored with it. The shops began to repeat themselves; very rarely now was there a type that he had not passed a little earlier in the day. What is more, that gnawing sensation, that at first had been faint, was becoming insistent and kept on growing in intensity. He had to do something to assuage it.

But what? He knew that stealing was wrong, but this knowledge puzzled him: if he did not know who or where he was, how could he know that stealing was wrong and, moreover, likely to get him into trouble?

He saw an arrow-shaped sign on a lamp-post consisting of a single white letter on a blue background: H. Somewhere in the recess of that vacuum, his mind, situated almost physically at the back of skull, this single letter stirred an unformed thought that acted like a burrowing insect in his brain. He stopped for a moment and stood still. H, what did H mean? He decided that he wouldn't move on until he had remembered, even if by standing there he drew attention to himself.

How does one drag things into consciousness? No one knows, of course, but suddenly the man had a flash of inspiration. Hospital, that was what H stood for. Anyone who was observing him closely would have noticed a slight widening of his eyes as he received this illumination; but no one was observing him closely. Why should they have been?

At last he had a goal to pursue, a direction to follow. He bent his steps in the direction indicated by the arrow. Before long, looming over the late Regency or early-Victorian terraces of which the area mainly consisted, there was a vast, grey concrete edifice of many floors and dull, dirty and mean-looking windows. It was the hospital. Another sign caught his attention: Accident and Emergency.

There was a long ramp where the ambulances arrived and an automatic door that opened with a rattle and a shudder when anyone approached it. On the ground outside was a crunchy carpet of discarded cigarette ends. 'Do I smoke?' wondered the man. He didn't know the answer.

He entered the building and not far inside was a counter with several women sitting behind it. Above them was a green sign with the word 'Reception'. The man approached the counter and, because it was not a busy time of day, there was no one in front of him. Nevertheless, the woman behind the counter immediately before him looked from her computer screen to the papers beside it, and back again, so that she did not notice, or at least attend to, him. He cleared his throat to draw her attention to his presence.

She looked up.

'Yes?' she said.

The man didn't know what to say. He had expected her to take the initiative.

She looked him up and down. He didn't look injured or even ill to her, and though not qualified in anything except paperwork, her experience had lent her a certain medical shrewdness, at least in her own opinion.

'What do you want?' She made it sound more like an accusation than a question, as if his object in being there were to waste her time.

'I need help,' said the man before her.

'What with?' asked the woman, disbelievingly.

The man realised that he could hardly say that he was hungry and penniless.

'I don't know who I am,' he said.

'We don't do psychotherapy here,' said the woman. 'This is accident and emergency.'

But in fact, much to her chagrin, she was not allowed to turn anyone away. It was this powerlessness, this lack of discretion, that provoked her asperity. When you have no choice but to give people what they want, you delight to deny it them as long as possible. In the circumstances, rudeness is self-respect.

Reluctantly, then, she turned to the computer to enter the man's details. Her hands hovered over the keyboard.

'Name?' she said.

'That's just it,' said the man. 'I don't know.'

The woman let out an exasperated sigh. How could he be fully conscious and yet not know his own name? She accepted, of course, that an unconscious man, knocked over in the street, might be brought to hospital without any identifying documents on him. Such a man could be recorded as 'Unknown Male,' and given a letter of the alphabet according to how many such unknown males had been found or picked up that day, though she had never known it get beyond the letter C because no one remained unidentified for long. Either the relatives or the police would claim the Unknown Male as their own; but it was clearly ridiculous to call a man standing upright before her, taking normally, Unknown Male B. Nevertheless, faced with no other choice, that is what she did.

'Date of birth?' she asked.

'I don't know that either,' said the man.

'Address?'

'I don't know,' said the man, adding by way of explanation that he couldn't remember anything until he woke up that morning.

'What do you mean, you can't remember anything?' said the receptionist. 'How did you get here?'

'I walked.'

'Where from?'

'I woke up in a cinema. I didn't know who I was or how I got there.'

The woman snorted in disapproval.

'Well, what do you want us to do about it?' she said. 'I have to put something down on the computer, otherwise you can't be seen.'

'I want to know who I am and where I came from,' said the man.

'This isn't a lost and found department, it's a hospital. Perhaps you should go to a lost property office, someone might be looking for you there.' She smiled at her own joke.

'I know,' said the man, 'but there must be something wrong with me if I can't remember nowt.'

'But what?' she replied. 'I have to put something down in writing.'

'Memory problems?' suggested the man in an almost supplicatory way.

'That's not on the system,' she snapped. 'It has to be something that's on the system, otherwise it won't record it.'

'I'm sorry,' said the man, but she did not accept his apology.

'You've given me a real problem,' she said. 'I'll have to think of something.' She stared ahead of her, as if trying to pluck a diagnosis from the void. 'Ah, that's it,' she said. 'Dementia, unspecified type.'

Her mood improved with the solution that she had found. Sometimes, after all, her job was rewarding.

'Go and sit over there,' she said, pointing to a waiting area. 'A doctor or nurse will be with you as soon as possible.'

The man went over to the waiting area and sat down. There was only one other person waiting there, a woman not yet old but with a face as wizened as a walnut. She smiled at the man as if welcoming him to a religious fellowship. Above them was a television screen, on which a sun-tanned man in his thirties, in a buttoned-up suit and a broad sky-blue tie, was speaking.

'Did the operation go badly?' he asked. 'Were you badly treated? Why not contact us? Remember, there's no fee to pay unless we win, so you have nothing to lose. Don't delay, contact us today.'

Another voice urged viewers to call o-eight-hundred, one three one three one four. Then a man appeared, dressed as a judge, and sang, with a ticker-tape of his words below him, 'Remember, where there's blame, there's a claim.'

Then the football resumed, as if it were a service essential to the running of the hospital. The commentator's words could not quite be made out, but his intonation was that of excitement, like a lunatic in a locked room.

'I don't really like this hospital,' said the woman to the man who was waiting with her. 'But it's the nearest.'

The man, now officially Unknown Male B, nodded.

'Most of the doctors are foreign. Sometimes you can't even understand what they're saying.'

The man nodded again.

'I've got a lump on my leg. What you here for?' asked the woman, who was clearly a regular.

'I don't know who I am,' said the man.

'You what?' she asked.

'I don't remember nowt from before this morning.'

The woman looked around her quickly.

'I think I'll just go and have a cup of tea,' she said, and moved away to the far side of a partition where he could not see her.

Two hours later a nurse emerged from somewhere in the interior of the hospital and, referring to a clipboard, called out 'Unknown Male B.' The man stood up.

'This way,' she said, and led him into a cubicle with a thin floral curtain around it and an examination within.

'Get undressed down to your underpants and the doctor will be with you shortly,' she said. 'Here's a gown for you.'

She handed him a flimsy gown that could be tied up at the back with bows, but not by the person wearing it.

About half an hour later the doctor entered the cubicle. He was concentrating intently on the documents he was holding as he entered. He put them aside after a short while.

'So you're the Unknown Mr B?' he said jocularly.

'That's what they call me.'

'Now why is that?' asked the doctor.

'I can't remember nowt until I woke up this morning. I don't even remember who I am.'

'Well, you're not from round here, to judge by your accent,' said the doctor. 'Let's take a good look at you.'

The doctor examined the man from head to foot, tapping his elbows, his knees and his ankles, shining a light in both his eyes, standing him upright with his eyes open and shut, and performing various other tests upon him. Having done all this, the doctor told him he could get dressed again.

'I can't find anything wrong with you,' said the doctor.

'There must be something,' said the man. 'I mean…'

'Anything physical,' said the doctor, unsure what to do next. He looked bemused, for he could hardly claim there was nothing at all wrong with a man who couldn't remember who he was. 'Are you sure you haven't had an accident, a bang on the head or something like that?'

The man repeated that he couldn't remember anything.

'I'm going to have to call someone else to examine you,' said the doctor. 'You'll have to wait here.'

The man waited for another two hours. He heard cries and groans coming from other cubicles. Young children wailed and a confused old lady cried 'No!' when the doctor did something

to her that she didn't like. All this held no interest for him, however; it passed over him like a mist; but when a nurse put her
head through the curtains that surrounded his cubicle, he mentioned that he was hungry.

'There's a vending machine on the other side,' she said.

'I haven't got no money,' the man said.

'I'm afraid that's too bad,' said the nurse. 'You'll have to wait
till you're admitted. We don't give out meals in A and E.'

At the end of the two hours, another doctor entered the
cubicle. He was casually, even shabbily dressed, and looked as
though the cares of the world weighed heavily on him.

'I'm a psychiatrist,' he said.

The man did not react as so many patients did, with surprise or shock. A man who is interested in nothing cannot be
surprised or shocked. His face registered no emotion.

The psychiatrist asked him a lot of questions, but he responded them like a man who has been arrested by the police
and stands on his right to remain silent. He didn't know when
or where he was born, who his parents were, where he went
to school, what his work was, if any, whether he was married
and had children, what his hobbies were, whether he had ever
had any illnesses or took medication, how much he drank or
whether he smoked cannabis. When the psychiatrist asked him
how old he was, he looked in the glass in the cubicle and said, 'I
look about forty.' He was trying to be helpful and co-operative,
not clever or cheeky; he did not want to appear deliberately ob-
structive.

'From your accent,' said the psychiatrist, 'you sound as if
you are from the North of England.'

But even this information evoked no response from the
man, to whom it meant nothing and for whom it jogged no
memory. He continued to look blankly at the psychiatrist.

'If you can't remember who you are,' said the psychiatrist,
'we'll have to admit you temporarily to the ward.'

The man looked neither pleased nor displeased. He seemed
detached from the world and even from his own life.

'I'll arrange for you to be transferred,' said the psychiatrist, 'and I'll see you later.'

The man waited another couple of hours in the cubicle. Eventually a porter arrived with a wheelchair. The porter was in a uniform that he had disarranged somewhat to demonstrate his individuality and to enter his protest against regimentation. His tie, loosened at his undone collar, hung at an angle to the vertical and displayed a rich pattern of stains. He wore running shoes that were out of keeping with the uniform, but which were not intended to convey an impression of expeditiousness, let alone athleticism. On the contrary, he moved as through an atmosphere that he found almost gelatinous. He had a rolled-up tabloid newspaper in the back pocket of his trousers.

He looked at the man and saw that he was not of the difficult, complaining or socially superior type.

'Come on mate,' he said, 'hop in.'

The man climbed down obediently from the examination couch. Apart from the fact that the flimsy gown was open at the back and it revealed his buttock, there was no reason why he could not have walked and had to be moved in a wheelchair.

The porter wheeled him along the corridor with his clothes piled on his lap. The passing parade of invalids, visitors, doctors in green gowns, nurses, patients pushing drip-stands, did not interest him.

'Are you a racing man?' asked the porter.

'A what?' said the man.

'A racing man. Do you follow the horses? The gee-gees?'

'I don't know.'

'You don't know?' The answer was so unexpected that the porter stopped pushing the wheelchair for a moment. 'You must know. I mean, either you do or you don't.'

'I can't remember nowt from this morning,' said the man.

The porter rolled his eyes heavenwards.

'Pity,' he said. 'I've got a dead cert for the 3.30 at Cheltenham.'

They reached the ward. A nurse in a dark uniform stood at the entrance.

'Put him in the end room,' she said to the porter.

The porter wheeled him through the ward, suddenly accelerating for no obvious reason. The other patients stared at him inquisitively. Those who were not too ill themselves took a lively interest in the illness of others, and perhaps even hoped for a tragedy, or at least a drama.

'I'm hungry,' said the man to a nurse who had come to take his details, having followed him the last few yards. 'Can I have something to eat?'

'It's too late now,' she said, as if he had dawdled on his way and had therefore to pay the price. 'There'll be something this evening.'

'Get up on the bed mate,' said the porter, and pulled the chair away from him as soon as he had stood up. 'See you.' And he went out, using the chair as a battering ram to open the swing doors.

The man got up on to his bed. A television at the end of an articulated arm like a spider-crab's limb hung over it, and relayed soundless images of a man in a leotard performing energetic callisthenics and obviously inviting the viewers to join in. The man pushed the screen away; then laid down on the bed, staring up at the ceiling composed of white polystyrene squares, one of which was coming loose and might suddenly fall on the bed. But the man was not frightened by the possibility.

He was left alone in the room for the rest of the day. The meal he had been promised turned out to be a couple of thin sandwiches, compressed as if by heavy weight, and a fibrous tangerine with a thick skin. The man felt by no means satisfied, and asked a cheerful Nigerian nurse who came in to take his pulse whether he could have a piece of toast.

'I'm sorry, my darling,' she said. 'I'm the only one on for the whole ward, and I don't have the time.'

So saying, she went to the ward office where she spoke on the telephone to a friend for half an hour about a party next week-end, and whether the handsome Dr Olugunde would go to it.

Somewhere in the ward a very old woman was crying out 'Nurse! Nurse! Help me! Help me!' But experience had shown that helping such old women did not stop them from crying out, and therefore she was ignored.

The psychiatrist came to the man's room the following day.

'How are you?" he asked. 'Remember anything yet?'

The man shook his head.

'I still can't remember nowt,' he said. 'I still don't know who I am.'

He seemed remarkably untroubled by his ignorance.

'We'll have to try to find out,' said the psychiatrist.

'How?' asked the man, a hint of anxiety entering his otherwise indifferent manner, as if the enquiry into his identity were a matter of mere academic interest.

'I want to try an injection,' said the psychiatrist. 'Of course, you have to agree to it.'

The man was in an awkward spot: he didn't want an injection, but didn't want to appear difficult either.

The psychiatrist put a printed form in front of the man. It had a lot of words on it and the man was not a great reader.

'What is it?' he asked.

'A consent form,' said the psychiatrist.

'What's that?'

'It says that I've explained everything to you and that you agree to it.'

He pushed a pen into the man's right hand – he assumed he was right-handed – and said, pointing to the bottom of the paper, 'Sign here.'

'But I don't know who I am,' said the man.

'Just put an X,' said the psychiatrist. 'I'll get someone to witness it.'

The man made such a mark.

'Right,' said the psychiatrist, 'what I'm going to do is to inject you with a drug that will make you feel very relaxed.'

'Why?' asked the man.

'Because that's what we do in cases like yours,' said the psychiatrist. 'When they don't recover spontaneously,' he added. 'Now lie back and I'll just clean your skin with this antiseptic.'

He wiped the crook of the man's arm with a little square

impregnated with alcohol, the coldness of which made the man start. 'And now a little pin-prick.'

The man looked down at what the psychiatrist was doing with a mild detached interest, as if it were being done to someone else, not himself. 'You might begin to feel a little sleepy,' said the psychiatrist.

And indeed he did. His head swam as if he had been suddenly whirled round and round; and his head as heavy as if it had been filled with lead shot, and it now took a supreme effort of will to move it a fraction in any direction. The psychiatrist's voice came to him as through a curtain of cotton wool.

'What's your name?' asked the psychiatrist.

'I... I don't know,' said the man, his speech now slurred and indistinct.

The psychiatrist pushed a little more of the drug into the man's vein, and his eyelids began to flicker. He was briefly asleep and then woke again.

The psychiatrist repeated the question a couple of times, but the only words that he could make out in reply were 'Don't know.'

The psychiatrist left off for a while as the man slipped into and out of a light and fitful sleep. Judging his moment, he asked him where he lived. The man muttered something, but so indistinctly that the psychiatrist did not catch it.

'Say that again,' he said. 'Where do you live?'

'Twenty-three...' muttered the man.

The psychiatrist's excitement rose, like a hunter closing in on his prey. He leaned forward, over the man's bed, so that he might catch every last syllable.

'Twenty-three where?'

'Twenty-three... twenty-three...' The man's voice faded, and he fell back into a light sleep.

The psychiatrist rubbed his forearm rhythmically to rouse waken him. The man came round a little.

'Twenty-three where?' asked the psychiatrist in a tone that in other circumstances would have been insidious.

'Twenty-three, Willow Street.'

The psychiatrist controlled himself. He knew that if he were impatient now, all might be lost.

'Twenty-three, Willow Street, where?' he asked slowly and gently, only just audibly, as if he did not really care if he received an answer.

'Twenty-three, Willow Street...'

'Yes?' said the psychiatrist.

'Twenty-three, Willow Street, Hindborough,' said the man, and then feel asleep exhausted by the effort of recollection.

The psychiatrist leapt to his feet, elated by his triumph. He left the man sleeping on the bed as if he were now surplus to requirement.

Hindborough, the town where the man lived, meant little to the psychiatrist other than it had a football team that had once been good but was so no longer, despite the town's fanatical devotion to it. The town, formerly industrial, was also known for its unemployment.

He was incurious to know more. Instead, he called the town's police and told the story of Unknown Male B who lived at twenty-three, Willow Street. Was a man known to be missing from there?

'Leave it with us, doctor,' said the policeman. 'We'll find out.'

The man, recovering quickly from the injection, was now staring up at the ceiling. About an hour later, the Hindborough police called the psychiatrist and told him that no one had been reported missing from that address. However, they would go round in person and check.

The psychiatrist was disappointed. Could it be that his self-congratulation was misplaced (he had positively crowed to the nurses)? But after another hour, during which time he was full of self-doubt, he had another call from the police.

'We've been to the house, doctor,' said the policeman, 'and a man has been missing from it for five days. It wasn't reported to us, that's why we didn't have a record of it. His name is John Jones and Mrs Jones lives at the same address.'

'Did you give her my number?'

'Yes, but she says, can you ring her? She says it's expensive for her to ring.'

The policeman gave him the number, which he called immediately. It rang for a long time and the psychiatrist was just about to conclude that there was no one in when a woman answered.

'Yes,' she said. Somehow she managed to convey deep mistrust and suspicion with a single syllable.

'Mrs Jones?' asked the psychiatrist.

'Yes. Who's that?'

'It's the hospital. We think we've got your husband here.'

'Quite possibly.'

'I understand he's been missing for a few days.'

There was a pause.

'Mrs Jones? Are you still there?'

'He often goes missing. This is the third time this year. Last time it was Glasgow. He does it whenever he's got something to tell me that I won't like, like he's lost his job because of his drinking. He was sacked a few days ago because he kept on being late for work.'

'I see. Well, we'll return him to you.'

'There's no rush,' she said. And she put the receiver down.

The psychiatrist returned to the man – now Mr John Jones – who was lying, neither contented nor discontented, on the bed. The psychiatrist sat down in the chair facing him.

'Does the name John Jones mean anything to you?' he asked. He looked intently into the man's face for the faintest change in expression, but there was none.

'No,' he said. Even the question itself did not interest him.

'You see,' said the psychiatrist, 'we think that's who you are. We've found your wife. You've been missing, apparently, for five days.'

'I can't say,' said the man. 'I don't remember nowt.'

'You don't remember losing your job a few days ago?'

'I don't remember nowt.'

'What work did you do?'

'I told you, I don't remember nowt.'

That was the nearest thing to an emotional response that the psychiatrist achieved.

'We'll take you back home,' he said.

'When?' asked the man, as if the question were an abstract one, of no personal significance.

'I can't say exactly.'

The psychiatrist immediately regretted having told him at all. He should have kept it to himself and sprung it on the man at the last moment, so there was no possibility of escape or a suicide attempt. Because of his indiscretion, he would have to arrange now that the man be specially watched by the staff, and they would not thank him for it.

But the man did not escape or try suicide; he had not even got off his bed, except to relieve himself.

Next day, quite early in the morning, a nurse came into his room. She had a raincoat over her uniform.

'Come on, John,' she said, 'we're going home.'

He slipped off the bed obediently.

'Where's that?' he asked.

'Hindborough, of course,' she said with a laugh.

He shook his head because it meant nothing to him.

'We've got a car waiting to take us to the station,' she said. 'We'd better hurry.'

They drove through the streets of the city, which had become busier and busier earlier and earlier to prove how important its activity was. But the animation passed by the man, who looked neither to his right nor to his left, but straight on, blankly. Did anything register with him? Impossible to tell. The driver grumbled about the traffic: there used to be a rush hour, but now it lasted all day.

They arrived at the station. A tidal wave of people, as expressionless as the man, was emerging from it, several commuter trains having just arrived. But even this the man, theoretically Mr Jones, did not appear to notice. He was like a fish swimming through a reef.

They boarded the train to Hindborough. It was quite a long journey, four hours at least. When he looked out of the windows of the carriage, his eyes flickered back and forth, but this was a physiological reaction rather than a sign of interest. The nurse quickly concluded that he had no conversation and took a glossy magazine from her bag, and began to read about the divorce of two celebrities, Shaz and Ravanna, because the latter had had a love-child by Stevie, a man so famous that any other name was superfluous.

They sped through landscapes both flat and hilly, through town and field, suburb and moorland, until eventually they approached the reddish-black-grey environs of Hindborough. It was built on some low hills overlooking the mouth of a river. Rising from the midst of rows of little terraced houses, dwarfing everything else, was a large stadium, its white cantilevers gleaming and its floodlights sticking up like the legs of an upturned insect.

'Ladies and gentlemen,' came a voice over the train's public address system, 'we are now approaching Hindborough, our final destination. Please remember to take all your belongings with you and watch your step as you alight on to the platform edge. We hope you had a pleasant journey and thank you for travelling with us today.'

'We're arriving,' said the nurse. 'Do you recognise it?'

The man made an effort to look out of the window.

'No,' he said, delivering an opinion as if it were the conclusion to a syllogism.

The train stopped in the station.

'Let's wait for everyone to get out,' said the nurse.

When the carriage had emptied, she said, 'Right, let's get off.'

She led him out on to the platform.

'Let's wait here,' she said. And they stood by the carriage from which they had just alighted.

The platform slowly cleared of people. After a few minutes, the only people left on it were themselves at one end and a woman with a children on either side of her at the other.

'Come on, let's go,' said the nurse. 'That must be your wife.'

They walked towards the woman and two children, who seemed rooted to the spot. But the immobility of the woman, thin as chain smokers are, was that of the coiled spring. As for the children, they were dressed in the gear of the local football team; their stillness was clearly momentary. Their anarchic activity was kept under control only by their mother's ability to scream at them.

Eventually the two parties came fact to face. The platform had seemed as if it stretched for miles.

'Mrs Jones?' asked the nurse.

'Yes,' she said. In the presence of a third party, she was restraining herself. And for the sake of appearances, she had to say something at least half-affectionate.

'Thank God you're home safe,' she said. 'We've been worried about you.'

He said nothing and she stepped forward to put her thin arms round his neck. The man stepped back a bit and said, 'Who are you.'

'I...'

'I don't think I've ever seen you before.'

The woman's face tightened like a knot tied by pulling two ends of a string.

'He can't come home like that,' she said to the nurse. 'I'm not having it. Not until he knows who he is. He'll have to go to Limetrees. They know him there.'

Limetrees was the local mental hospital built in what was once the countryside but was now in a suburb of Hindborough. Its grounds were the only open space for miles around.

'They won't know he's coming,' said the nurse. 'We can't just turn up like that.'

'It's all right,' said Mrs Jones. 'They know him of old there. He does this regularly. Last time they did all kinds of tests in Glasgow though I told them it wasn't necessary and that he would get better after a day or two in Limetrees. A right waste of time and money, I call it.'

'So what do you suggest I do?' aske the nurse.

'Take him there – leave him on the doorstep if you like.'

'Are you coming with?'

'Coming with? What for? I've no money to waste on taxis and who'd look after the kids? No, lass, you'll have to take him there yourself. Come on, kids.'

So saying, she grabbed the children by their hands, turned round and yanked them in the direction of the station exit.

'Bye, dad,' said the two children as they went, 'see you in a bit.'

The man and his nurse were left on the station platform, like flotsam on a beach after the tide has receded. The man's expression had not changed: it was still blank.

'I suppose we'll have to do as your wife suggests,' said the nurse, leading him to the taxi rank. The man made no objection.

Limetrees, formerly the Hindborough Asylum for the Insane and Feebleminded, was a large Gothic-style building with a central tower and workhouse wings. In front of it was a cricket pitch on which the annual match between staff and patients used to be played. Just inside the main entrance was a glass-fronted booth that served as reception and telephone exchange. The man behind the counter was a man who had worked there for years – his whole life – and knew the patients better than any of the doctors. As soon as he saw the man his face lit up in recognition.

'Hello, John, back again? Couldn't keep away, huh? It must be the food. I'll call Dr Bell to tell him you've come back.' He turned to the nurse. 'Why don't you take a seat, my love. Would you like a cup of tea? Milk and sugar?'

Mr Jones was admitted to a ward under his own name, though he did not as yet not acknowledge it. The nurse left him.

He recovered his memory, all of a sudden, like a clearing reached in a forest, two days later, after a young lunatic under the influence of cannabis brought a fire extinguisher down on the shoulder of an old woman who was suicidal after the death of her husband from cancer. He had been aiming for her head.

As soon as he recovered his memory, Mr Jones went to the nurses, who were having their morning break. He knocked on their door: he could see them through the glass partition.

'Wait a moment, John,' said the head nurse. 'We're busy just at the moment.'

The nurses were always busy, as a matter of principle. But after a decent interval, one of them stepped out of the office.

'Yes, John, what is it?' she asked.

'I've got my memory back,' he said, smiling. 'I can remember everything now, clear as anything. I'm ready for home.'

He couldn't leave straight away because the doctor had to agree to it as well. And then, because he had no money, a bus-fare had to be found for him. He left Limetrees towards the end of the afternoon.

He walked up Willow Street, with its parallel row of identical small dwellings. He reached number twenty-three and knocked on its door.

The door opened with an angry clatter and Mrs Jones stood on the doorstep with her hands on her hips.

'Hello, love,' he said. 'I've recovered. I'm better now.'

'Who are you?' she asked. 'I don't think I've ever seen you before.'

And the door slammed shut in his face.

- 7 -
The Cure

WHEN MR AZIZ had his heart attack he decided to retire not only from his shop but from all activity whatsoever: unless getting out of bed, sitting in his chair all day reading the paper, calling frequently to his wife for a sweet and milky cup of tea and eating the meals she placed before him be counted as activity.

Mr Aziz said that, try as he might, anything more strenuous was impossible for him and brought on a pain in his chest: the harbinger, if not the cause, of another, possibly fatal heart attack.

For the first few weeks after his return home from the hospital, Mrs Aziz, mother of his seven grown-up children, attended assiduously to his every wish. Of course she had always done so; it was not so much her job as her role in life, a destiny. Anything else would have been unthinkable for her, but before his heart attack Mr Aziz had spent more than fourteen hours a day in his shop, closing it only when there was not the faintest possibility of another customer, and therefore Mrs Aziz had had little to do for him. It was by working so hard that Mr Aziz, who had started from nothing, was able to buy a house for each of his children.

Then, six weeks after her husband's heart attack, Mrs Aziz, who had always been too busy looking after the children ever to be ill, began to weaken. More exactly, her right leg began to refuse to obey her command. At first, this was only intermittent, but even so it caused a lot of trouble when Mr Aziz called for a cup of tea and she couldn't bring it. Then she would call out to him from another room that she couldn't move because of her leg; Mr Aziz, never a patient man, grew angry rather than solicitous and began to shout (which wasn't good for his heart). But strangely enough this did not produce the required effect, as it always had done before; indeed, it seemed only to make Mrs Aziz's leg all the weaker and less obedient to her command.

Mr Aziz, who believed that he had a right to his bad temper because of all his hard work, was so angry that he almost got out of his chair; but he started to worry when his meals, and not just his tea, failed to appear.

Yes, there really was something wrong with his wife. The most obvious explanation was sorcery or a *djinn*, but when he told his eldest son, Ahmed, a chartered accountant, he replied that Mrs Aziz needed a doctor more than the imam. His son admitted, of course, that the ultimate source of the weakness was probably a malign neighbour or *djinn*, but even they had to work through the body, about which doctors these days knew a great deal.

Nevertheless, Mr Aziz called the imam first. The latter, a middle-aged man with a sparse beard dyed with henna, prayed over her vigorously, took some money afterwards, but failed to cure her. Her leg was now so obdurate that his daughters had to come to look after their father, or he would have starved.

Eventually Mr Aziz asked the doctor to visit her; but Dr Akhtar said that if she wasn't well enough to come to his surgery, she should go straight to the hospital. Mr Aziz got his son to call for an ambulance.

It was Ahmed who accompanied her to the hospital, Mr Aziz not being well enough to go. He walked beside the ambulance men who carried her on a stretcher into the vehicle, and he climbed in beside her.

By the time Mrs Aziz reached the hospital, she seemed to have shrunk, as if she had been desiccated en route. Her shawl seemed too large for what it had to cover; there were square yards of unused cloth. Her personality had shrunk along with her body; normally quite forceful with her children, and possessed of her own ideas when she was alone with them, she was now timid and frightened. She had become a little old lady in a matter of minutes.

Lifted on to a trolley, her right leg now quite useless, more a ball and chain than a limb, she was wheeled into a curtained cubicle in the emergency department, her son always beside her. And there they waited for three quarters of an hour, listening to, or at any rate hearing, the sounds of a child crying when told it needed stitches, or the shouts of an early drunk resisting what was proposed to him for his own good.

Eventually a young doctor burst through the curtains surrounding Mrs Aziz and her son. He was dressed in a thin green tunic and trousers.

'You're her son,' he said to Ahmed without looking at Mrs Aziz.

'Yes,' he said.

'She doesn't speak English, I suppose,' said the doctor.

'No.'

A look of exasperation flitted across the doctor's face. Forty years in the country and hardly a word learnt!

'You'll have to interpret for me. Our interpreter's off on another case. Maternity. Twins.'

He looked at Mrs Aziz for the first time.

'What's wrong?' he asked.

'My leg,' said Mrs Aziz hesitantly, and with a strong accent.

'It's her leg,' said Ahmed. 'It's gradually stopped working.'

'When did she first notice it?' asked the doctor.

The doctor took a lot of details from Ahmed, and then said, 'Tell her I'm going to examine her.'

This simple message seemed to the doctor to take a very long time to convey. Perhaps there was no word for 'examine' in her language. She answered her son back as if they were arguing. She sounded querulous in a weak way.

'I'll call in a chaperone,' said the doctor, and went out of the cubicle, returning with a fat and jolly black woman, who treated life as an extended joke.

'Just step outside for a few moments,' said the doctor to Ahmed.

When he had finished, he called Ahmed back in.

'I haven't found anything,' said the doctor. 'I'm going to call a neurologist. Can you explain that to her?'

'Neurologist' appeared to be another word for which there was no equivalent in her language. After several minutes of dialogue, Ahmed turned to the doctor.

'She says thank you,' he said.

'You're welcome,' said the doctor, already halfway through the curtains; and a wait, this time more prolonged, ensued.

Another doctor entered, slightly older and differently attired. He wore a blue chalk-striped suit and a yellow bow tie, though he was not yet at the pinnacle of the profession.

'Mrs Aziz?' he asked.

'Yes,' she replied hesitantly.

'I've come to the right place, then,' he said, laughing slightly. He exuded charm, like a secretion.

In essence, however, he went through the same procedure, asked the same questions as the previous doctor, only a little more thoroughly. And at the end, he pronounced himself unsatisfied: Mrs Aziz would have to be admitted to the ward for further tests.

Ahmed agreed on her behalf and she was wheeled up to a ward. There were five other people in it, thankfully women, all of them older than she, four of whom had had strokes, one of whom flailed her arm and grunted like a bellows, and a fifth whose illness left her face blank and made it difficult for her to move. She, as it happened, spoke a language not dissimilar from that of Mrs Aziz, but unfortunately she was the adherent of a bad religion, hostile to that of Mrs Aziz, so there was no one for her to speak to, or to speak to her once Ahmed had to leave.

In the days that followed Mrs Aziz was subjected to every possible test and investigation. Being in hospital for her was like war for an infantryman: ninety-nine per cent boredom, and one per cent terror, the latter when she was rolled on her back into giant machines. Everything was explained to her in a language she could not understand; only once the interpreter came to explain things to her, but she was also of a bad religion and did not like Mrs Aziz, telling her that she should try harder to walk.

At visiting time all her children came, though never her husband, for he was too ill to do so; they brought her tasty things to eat to make up for the hospital food which was like wet cement mixed with paper. Ahmed was always their spokesman, and asked to speak to the doctor.

It was only at the fourth time of asking that the doctor came: different from the others that Ahmed had met. She was young and blonde and spoke with a lisp. Her manner was awkward, but at the same time a little aggressive.

'We can't find anything wrong with your mother,' she said.

'Well, there must be something wrong with her,' said Ahmed. 'She can't move her leg. She can't walk.'

'When I said we can't find anything wrong with your mother,' said the doctor, 'I mean nothing physical. The scans don't show anything that could explain her paralysis.'

'Then why can't she move her leg?' asked Ahmed.

'I agree she can't move her leg,' said the doctor. 'But the question is why?'

'Yes,' said Ahmed. 'That's why she's here.'

'Is there anything that could be upsetting her?' asked the doctor.

'What d'you mean?'

'Well, something that's on her mind?'

'Like what?'

'I don't know. A problem, something like that?'

'What kind of problem?'

'I don't know. A money problem perhaps.'

'There's no money problem. She has everything she wants. There's plenty of money. Anyway, how could a money problem mean she couldn't walk? There must be something wrong with her.'

'I'm not saying there's nothing wrong with her, I'm just trying to find out what it might be.'

'Something physical, I mean.'

'Well you see, we haven't been able to find anything.'

'Does that mean it couldn't be there?'

'It makes it very unlikely.'

'You never make mistakes, you never miss anything?'

'No, I wouldn't say that,' said the doctor. 'But all the same…'

'I mean, she's never had a day's illness in her life, and then suddenly she can't walk and you're telling me there's nothing wrong with her?'

'I'm not saying there's nothing wrong with her, I'm just saying there's nothing physical causing it.'

'You mean she's mad?'

'No, not mad, worried perhaps. Something wrong in the family, perhaps?'

'There's nothing wrong in the family. We've always been a happy, close family. If you don't believe me, you can ask the others. They're all here.'

Ahmed left the room to fetch the others. Soon they all trooped in.

'The doctor asked whether there was anything wrong in the family,' he said. He was clearly the most senior of them, both in age and accomplishment. 'She said it could be causing our mother's paralysed leg. I said that there wasn't anything wrong. We've always been a normal happy family, haven't we, and we still are. You can ask anyone in our community as well.'

The others murmured their agreement. Two of them looked angry at the suggestion.

'So you see,' said Ahmed to the doctor.

'Nevertheless…' said the doctor.

'You'd better do more tests,' he said.

'We've done them all. There aren't any more to do.'

'There must be. After all, she still can't walk.'

'No, she can't walk, but the question is…'

'Can we take her to another hospital? A private one. We can easily afford it.'

'It's not a question of money. We've done all the necessary

tests and we can't find anything wrong physically to account for her symptoms.'

'But we can take her if we want?'

'Of course. No one can stop you. But you'd be wasting your money.'

'Good. That's what we'll do.'

It took a little time to arrange, but Mrs Aziz went. The new hospital was smaller and quieter. Mrs Aziz had her own room, she could watch films in it in her own language. They asked her what she wanted to eat, and they brought her something that faintly resembled what she had at home. It was quite comfortable.

They put her through the same tests, though. But this time she was less frightened, both because the staff were more solicitous, even if they couldn't speak her language, and because she'd had them before and knew what to expect. When Ahmed asked to see the doctor, he came at once.

He was dressed like the second doctor in the other hospital, but the clothes were more natural to him. He seemed to flow up from the floor in a graceful arc, like a seller of fine arts. He was both friendly and distant, combining the two by some alchemy of his own.

'I'm very glad to say that we haven't found any serious structural abnormalities in your mother's nervous system, and therefore I think she's going to recover completely. In fact, I think she's improving already.'

'What was wrong with her?' asked Ahmed.

'Wrong with her? It's not possible to say exactly. In my opinion, she probably had a virus. Sometimes people get paralyses after a viral infection, for reasons that we don't yet fully understand. At least ninety-five per cent of such cases recover fully, and I think your mother will be among them.'

'Why didn't the other hospital tell us that?' asked Ahmed.

The doctor smiled with just a hint of sadness.

'It is not always an easy diagnosis to make, and only becomes clear with the passage of time.'

'So what happens now?' asked Ahmed.

'The problem is that your mother has been so long in bed that she has what we call disuse atrophy of her muscles. That is muscle wasting in layman's language. She has to be taught how to use them again so that they can be built back up and return to normal.'

'How's that done?'

'She has to undergo intensive rehabilitation, with lots of physiotherapy. She might also need occupational therapy, to get her back to what she was doing before.'

'How long will it take?' Ahmed was nervous, because the hospital was costing a fortune.

The doctor looked Ahmed in the eye. His assessments were quick.

'Well,' he said, 'in my opinion she could be just as well rehabilitated in the other hospital as in this. It might be a waste of your money for her to stay here.'

Ahmed could not control the smile that spread on his face.

'Thank you, doctor,' he said. 'We're all very grateful to you.'

Mrs Aziz returned to the first hospital, to a ward where those who had had strokes were taught to walk or speak again. Some even had to be taught to eat, for when they tried the food either came out of the sides of their mouth or went down the wrong way and started to choke them. The ward smelt of urine.

A large Australian girl, bouncing with optimistic energy and strength, came to Mrs Aziz, who was lying in bed. She was a physiotherapist.

'Come on, Jamila,' she said. 'Rise and shine.'

Mrs Aziz looked puzzled. She hadn't understood.

'It's time to get out of bed,' said the physiotherapist.

'I'm tired,' said Mrs Aziz. 'Tomorrow better.'

But the physiotherapist was used to excuses and procrastination.

'Never mind. We'll get you out in the chair first.' And she pulled the bedclothes from Mrs Aziz's recumbent form.

Mrs Aziz was soon in the chair. She had not so much moved as been moved into it. Then the physiotherapist, on one knee, started to bend Mrs Aziz's paralysed leg. Mrs Aziz screamed, though decorously.

'Aw come on, Jamila,' said the physiotherapist. 'That didn't hurt a bit.' And the bending grew more vigorous.

'Tomorrow,' said the physiotherapist, looking at her watch, 'we'll take our first step. You don't want to be stuck here forever, do you?'

When she had gone, Mrs Aziz called for the nurse.

'Bed,' she said, pointing to it.

'No,' said the nurse. 'Not before bedtime. You've got to stay out of bed till then.'

Mrs Aziz hadn't the words to argue, but in any case there was a tone of finality in the nurse's voice. How cruel they were here, how lacking in understanding!

Nights were actually the worst time, even though Mrs Aziz was in bed, for two of the patients in the ward screamed 'Nurse! Nurse!' for hours on end. When the nurse came – which wasn't often – they couldn't explain what they wanted and resumed their screams straight after she left. Sleep was impossible.

So when the physiotherapist came and said that the more she practised walking, the sooner she would be out of the hospital, Mrs Aziz began to see the sense of it. Her resistance changed to cooperation; sometimes, indeed, the nurses had to prevent her from walking with her stick out of the ward into the corridor outside.

'What would happen if you fell?' they said. Happen to us, they meant. Mrs Aziz had to content herself with walking in confines of the ward.

She was so well that the staff began to speak of her returning home. First, though, they had to make sure that she would be able to manage there. A young woman came up to her as she was walking in the ward.

'Hello,' she said. 'I'm Sarah, the occupational therapy student. I've come to do an assessment.'

She led Mrs Aziz into a large room off the ward where Mrs Aziz had not been before. There was a plastic-topped table and some plastic chairs in the middle, and on the far side a stainless-steel sink unit and a gas cooker. Sarah watched Mrs Aziz clean some plates and then boil two kettles, first an electric one and then one on the gas cooker. She remembered to turn the gas off and had no difficulty in pouring the hot water into a teapot and a mug.

'It's all right,' said Sarah jovially. 'I won't ask you to make sandwiches. I don't suppose you have them at home.'

Mrs Aziz was now ready for discharge from the hospital. Ahmed, wreathed in smiles, came to fetch her. The staff, in truth not accustomed to such total success, had become fond of her, and lined up to wave goodbye to her.

On the way home, Ahmed explained how the doctors had told him that it would be best if Mrs Aziz resumed her normal activities at once because she might have a relapse if she didn't. But one at least of the children would visit every day to make sure that everything was all right.

When they arrived home, Mr Aziz was having a snack of tea and barfi. He grunted when she arrived because his mouth was full. And because of his heart, he did not get up.

It was surprising how well Mrs Aziz managed in the first two days. She cooked pilau rice and several vegetable curries to go with it (Mr Aziz had been told to cut down on meat). She served them to her husband on a tray that he balanced on his knees. Since she used so many spices in the cooking, it was only natural that the balance between them was not quite right for Mr Aziz's taste: a little more of this, or a little less of that, would have been better.

Ahmed came on the third day after her discharge from hospital. He had his own key to the house and let himself in. He knew at once that there was something wrong, or at any rate different. The silence had a kind of density to it, it was almost like a physical resistance.

He walked into the room where his father had sat every day since his heart attack. He was in the chair all right, with the green and black felt picture of the Kaba still on the wall above him, but he was slumped sideways. Blood soaked his grey kurta pyjama. There was blood on the floor too, with a large kitchen knife. Mr Aziz stared sightlessly into infinity.

Ahmed called out for his mother, breaking the silence as a fragile stone fractures under a blow. Unlike the stone, however, the silence re-established itself.

Ahmed went into the kitchen. There was no one there. Then he rushed up the stairs into the bedroom. His mother was on the bed staring up at the ceiling. She didn't turn towards him when he entered. And not only her right leg, but her right arm was completely paralysed.

- 8 -
Treatment for a King

KING REGINALD, the First of that Name, sat down in his throne-room, previously known to his neighbours and his few visitors as his lounge, and began to write a letter. His royal palace, postal address 23, Magnolia Drive, Forehampton, was of course only his temporary residence, until such time as the Usurpers vacated his rightful abode in London.

The blank page before him, he hesitated: how to address the recipient of his stern missive? She, the intended recipient, had played her part for so long now that she probably had forgotten that she was a fraud, an interloper, an actress. He decided to address her as Mrs Windsor, though on the envelope he would put Mrs Elizabeth Windsor so that there could be no mistake as to whom it was addressed and no excuse for failure to deliver it.

'Dear Mrs Windsor,' he began, but then paused, his pen hovering over paper. What tone should he adopt? Naturally he was angry, as anyone who had been cheated of his birthright would be. But King Reginald, the First of that Name, was in general a mild-mannered man who slid away from conflict by some kind of social lubrication. And also being at heart a kind man, he understood that, after all these years, it might not be easy for Elizabeth Windsor to move out of the property she wrongfully occupied or abandon her false position that had, from sheer force of habit, become true in her mind. She was now an old woman and had begun her charade at the age of twenty-six. All the same, justice was justice, the law was law, and his right was his right. Did not his escutcheon say, *Dieu et mon droit?* A certain firmness was therefore called for, without aggression or, in the first instance, threat. Stronger language might be necessary later.

'We, Reginald,' the royal writer continued, 'by the Grace of God King of the United Kingdom of Great Britain and Northern Ireland, having been informed that you, Mrs Elizabeth Windsor, and your family and followers, having been in wrongful occupation of several of our palaces throughout our realm, do hereby request and require that you, Mrs Elizabeth Windsor, your family and followers, do vacate the said palaces by a date not later than fourteen (14) days from the date of this Royal Letter, in which case you and your family and followers, staff and servants, will receive our Royal Pardon.'

His Majesty sat back and read, not without a certain admiration for his own temperance, what he had written.

'Yes,' he thought, 'I think that strike the right tone. Firm, not bullying.'

Strange to relate, although he had been a royal personage since birth (as all true royal personages were), this was the first letter he had ever written in his royal capacity. Equally strange to relate, though he had been born royal, he had not realised it until about three days before. On that day, everything had suddenly become clear to him. For about two weeks beforehand, he had been feeling oddly exalted without being able to put his finger on exactly why. Then, on that day, he had been looking out of his front window when a large black Rolls-Royce went by, followed by several large black saloon cars. He knew at once that it was a sign: it meant that he was King and was meant not to ride in any other vehicle than the large and stately Rolls-Royce. The reason for his previous exultation was now clear to him. It had been justified all along: his instinct had been right.

Before he was aware that he was King of England (though looking back on his life from his current state of awareness, he had always suspected that there was something different, predestined about him) King Reginald, the First of that Name, had been known as Smith, an excellent alias in so far as it could not better have concealed his identity. His job, too, had concealed it well: librarian at Forehampton Branch Library. But his name Reg, as he was sometimes known there, had surely always included some sly and self-deprecating etymological reference to his regal status?

Two weeks before his exaltation began, he had received a circular informing him that, because of budgetary considerations, the Forehampton branch library was soon to close. At first this news upset him deeply; for although the work was not too strenuous, he believed he had made a significant contribution to the cultural life of the town, for example by setting up a Nature corner in the library for its children. And if the library closed, where would the old widowers with nowhere else to go now go?

But with the exaltation came the understanding that he was born to something grander than to advise elderly women on which of the latest crime novels to read (which he had not read himself) and to tell children to keep their voices down because this was a library. The closure was surely a sign of Destiny rather than a setback for it came just at an opportune moment. He had taken that destiny into his own hands.

It was easy enough to sign his letter Reginald R - Reginald Rex - but how to post it? It would have been best, of course, to seal it with wax and a seal, to demonstrate that it was no ordinary missive, but it was difficult these days to find such wax anywhere and impossible in Forehampton. Instead, he wrote OHMS - On His Majesty's Service - in large red letters on the flap of the envelope. That should be sufficient to let the usurper and her servitors know that it was important.

His Majesty took the letter to the post office pondering as he passed the semi-detached houses en route whether he should send it recorded delivery. Surely the OHMS by itself should be enough to secure delivery? On the other hand, the fact that someone signed for its receipt would be an implicit acknowledgement by the Usurper (who now had a capital letter in his mind) that Mrs Elizabeth Windsor was her true name and the correct form of address. If ever it came to a case in court this would be evidence.

He walked down Magnolia Drive, letter in hand, and turned into Forsythia Way, which itself led into the High Street in which was situated the post office. The time was fast approaching, of course, when he would no longer have to perform himself such menial tasks as posting a letter: there would be footmen, secretaries and chamberlains to do the like. But such had been the success of the Usurpation – another capital letter – that he had been deprived of his most elementary rights and privileges as a royal person. That was why he forgave people in the street for their failure to bow or curtsey to him as he passed. They had been deliberately kept in ignorance, as indeed had he until very recently. The Usurpation had been cunning, ruthless and thorough. It had infiltrated its lies and falsities everywhere and so the people were not to be blamed for their lack of respect.

For the moment, however, it was probably best not to enlighten them, and to let them go on thinking that he was Reginald Smith, librarian and wearer of a worn tweed jacket with leather patches. There would be time enough for them to render him the due homage and to regret their previous over-familiarity and impudence towards him. How embarrassed they would be: but he would be gracious. He would rise above his anger at their previous insolence.

The lady at the post office counter took his letter as if it were just any other rather than an historic document that would change the country's history. Naturally there was no way she could have known this but even the address, Buckingham Palace, London SW1, did not raise her eyebrow. As someone who himself had long had dealings with the public, however, His Majesty was fully aware that some of his subjects were not quite twelve pence to the shilling and in effect sleep-walked their way through life.

There was nothing further to be done now that he had posted the letter, other than to wait, at least for a time. Although he was a sovereign deprived of his rights – and that since birth –

His Majesty did not want to appear impatient, unreasonable or over-eager. *Noblesse oblige*, after all.

But how many days would it be reasonable to wait? If he didn't want to appear hurried, as a parvenu might, neither could he afford to let things slide as if unsure of his rightful claim, as if he were just trying it on. Were not the words *Dieu et mon droit* inscribed on his coat of arms? He decided that four days was long enough before he sent something more strongly worded, like successive warnings over library books not returned on time.

The four days were now up. All that had come through the letterbox in the meantime were offers of cut-price insurance for his water-pipes and drainage, and a flyer for the Liberal-Democrat candidate in the forthcoming local elections, promising to build a youth centre for the youth of Forehampton who had nothing to do, thereby preventing them from smashing bus shelters.

It was time for another letter. His Majesty would have now to harden his tone. Some people – usurpers among them - did not listen to reason. It was all very well for the Bible to say that a soft answer turned away wrath, but had it ever been known to persuade a usurper to desist and repent?

'Dear Mrs Windsor,' he began again, 'It appears that you have chosen to to ignore our previous letter demanding your evacuation of our Royal Palace.' (He was not quite accustomed to using the royal first person, and realised that he would have to maintain his vigilance in order not to slip back into the singular, which his enemies might use to dispute his claims). 'We therefore require and command you on receipt of the Royal Instruction, without further prevarication or procrastination, to vacate our Royal Palace, and all our other Royal Palaces, within twenty-four hours. Given this day under our hand, Reginald R.'

It was true, thought the King, that at first sight such a letter might seem surprising addressed from 23, Magnolia Drive, Forehampton, but had not Charles II taken refuge in an oak tree and was not 23, Magnolia Drive, somewhat grander and more commodious than an oak tree? A king is king by virtue of his birth, not by that of his current residence; it is possible to be regal in a pigsty. Nor is a king a king by virtue of what he does or how he behaves, though of course it is better if he behaves well. One is either born a king or not, and Reginald had been so born. His only regret was that his mother, the late Queen Mother, Queen Doris, had never lived to see the day of her restoration. His first act would be to remove her remains from Forehampton Municipal Cemetery to the Royal Chapel at Windsor.

His Majesty waited another three days: again, there was silence. Real firmness was now required.

King Reginald, the First of that Name, had not slept more than fitfully for the last four nights, kept awake by making plans for his coronation and how to evict the Usurpers by force if it were needed. He might have to go to the palace in person to arrest them all: for if a mere citizen were entitled by the law to make an arrest, surely a rightful sovereign had the same right?

'You, Elizabeth Windsor,' he next wrote, 'are hereby commanded to vacate our Royal Palace forthwith, or face the consequences. We remind you that the death penalty is still in force for the crime of treason.'

This time he sent the letter both express and recorded delivery.

The following day, at two o'clock in the afternoon, there was a knock on his front door. His Majesty opened the door himself and saw a policemen standing in front of him. He assumed that he had arrived to escort him in glory to the Palace, his rightful home: the policeman looked a little surprised to be confronted by His Majesty himself instead of a footman.

'Good afternoon, sir,' said the policeman, politely enough for the ordinary citizen, but hardly appropriate for his sovereign.

'Don't you mean *Your Majesty*?' asked the King, with a faint touch of asperity.

The policeman gave no sign of having heard.

'Are you Reginald Smith?' he asked.

'That is the alias by which I have long been known,' replied the King, again with a faint *hauteur*.

Another policeman appeared from behind the thriving ley-landia that grew between His Majesty's front garden and the road.

'I arrest you on a charge of...'

The King did not quite catch the nature of the charge – or rather, the so-called charge. Obviously, the Usurpers would stop at nothing, no depths they would not descend to, in the attempt to preserve their position.

'You are committing treason,' His Majesty said, as one of the policemen, in a swift movement, clamped handcuffs round his wrists so that they came together almost as if in an act of prayer.

'Now we don't want any trouble, do we?' said one of the policemen.

The King decided that regal dignity would be best, even if it were injured. Did not Shakespeare himself say that the whirligig of time would bring in its revenges? Did not Charles I go the scaffold with such grace that the people who saw it fell to their knees?

It was also necessary to be realistic. What chance did a man who had spent years as a branch librarian have against two policemen? There had sometimes been awkward customers at the library, but never any requiring physical force to remove, which he would have been unqualified and unable to apply in any case. Again, there would be time enough to punish those responsible, among whom (he thought, pleased with his own magnanimity and largeness of spirit) were not the policemen, who thought they were only doing their job, under the ultimate direction of the Usurpers. When you looked into their faces, you saw that they were not very intelligent; and His Majesty had always thought that the dictum that ignorance was no excuse for breaking the law was unduly harsh.

Still, there was no reason for them to bundle their sovereign so roughly into the waiting white police van. His Majesty, no *aficionado* (yet) of motor vehicles had never been in one so uncomfortable. It was a strange introduction to royal luxury. He was pushed down on to a cold metal bench that ran along the inside of the windowless rear of the van, with the two policemen on either side of him restricting his movements. His Majesty thought that this was no way to treat anyone, let alone him, and he made a mental note of it as the first reform to be undertaken in his reign.

The van, driven by a third policeman who had been waiting all along, seemed to careen and career through the streets, for reasons that he literally could not see. He began to feel slightly seasick (not that he had been to sea). The van was obviously speeding at the top of its capacity, to judge by the engine noise; but what was the hurry? Although he could see nothing, a blue light flashed rhythmically though the semi-gloom of the van's interior. It was as if it were an emergency, which perhaps for the Usurpers it was. His letters must have frightened them into taking counter-measures before their content leaked out and caused unrest. People did not like to have been duped, especially for so long a period.

The van arrived at the police station. It had not been a long journey because nowhere in Forehampton was very far from anywhere else. The back doors of the van were thrown open with what seemed like violence.

'Out you get,' said a voice roughly and without any ceremony.

His Majesty stood, but though not a tall man he hit his head on the ribbing of the van's roof.

'Careful!' said the voice. 'Watch where you go!'

The voice was not solicitous, at least not of him. It implied that any accident that befell him would be his own fault. As he reached the van doors, now open wide, his forearm was suddenly gripped and he was hauled down a couple of steps stumbling as he emerged into the light. He was led into the station via a back door. Until then he had not known there was a back door to Forehampton police station.

The custody sergeant behind the desk was clearly a cut above the other policemen. The King was relieved to discover that not everything malfunctioned under the Usurpers, that some men were still promoted on the grounds of merit.

'Are you Reginald Smith, of 23, Magnolia Drive?' asked the sergeant.

Should he reveal his true identity? One should not tell lies.

'That is how people know me,' he replied, pleased with his own deftness in avoiding untruth while reserving his position.

'How do you feel, all right?'

Not suicidal, if that's what you're thinking, thought His Majesty. King's may abdicate, but not by suicide. Before he could say anything, however, a crackly voice came over a radio, indecipherable to His Majesty, but not to the sergeant.

'I better see to that,' said the sergeant, and turned to the other policemen. 'Put him into number three for now,' adding that he did not think that the suspect needed to be cuffed.

One of the policemen stepped forward and released his wrists.

'Come along,' he said.

His Majesty was led along a stone corridor, painted chocolate brown up to knee-level and dirty cream above, and shown into a cell. A steel door with a judas-window clanged shut behind him, echoing down the corridor.

Ahead of him, affixed to the wall, was a concrete slab the size and shape of a bed. High above it was a small rectangular window with bars, which gave out on to the grey sky. Scratched on to the paint of the wall were the words of a previous occupant of the cell: Fuck the police, fuck the world!

His majesty sat down on the concrete slab. From another cell nearby, echoing, came the voice of a detained drunk pounding his fists on the steel door: a mixture of rage, levity and demands for release.

A policeman opened the cell door bearing a chipped enamel mug with sweet milky tea. He held it out towards His Majesty.

'Here you are, mate,' he said.

Mate! Was that any way to address a reigning monarch, let alone one's own? But His Majesty swallowed the insult because it was not intended as an insult and was the product of ignorance rather than impudence. Besides, once he was settled on the throne, the story of how he had so meekly borne the treatment to which he had been subject would emerge, and his subjects would regard him with all the more affection and loyalty. The unexalted like the modest.

The policeman withdrew – without bowing, of course, but nevertheless proceeding backwards. This may have been because one should not turn one's back on prisoners who are still unknown quantities.

The tea was disgusting, proletarian: but again, it was probably to His Majesty's advantage that he should be able to say that he knew about, had experienced and survived the conditions in which so many of his subjects lived.

Shortly afterwards he was brought a sandwich of sliced white bread whose edges had curled up and dried at the corners, containing a cold sausage sliced lengthways down the middle. This, too, was valuable experience for a future monarch to be able to say that he had had, for it would refute the allegations of malcontents that he had been born with a silver spoon in his mouth and did not know how the common people lived and ate.

After the sandwich, he was brought a rough prickly blanket, a little like a hair shirt, and told to try to get some rest, as if a siesta after a sliced sausage were the most natural thing in the world. And indeed, the noisy drunk in the cell nearby, began to snore stertorously, though not because of the sandwich, which he had thrown through the judas-window when it had been briefly opened, and not because it disgusted him but as a matter of principle.

His Majesty did lie down, but only because there was nothing else to do. Before long, however, the cell door was unlocked (was it really necessary to make so much noise about it?) and a policeman entered.

'The doctor's here to see you,' he said.

The doctor? His Majesty was not ill and had not requested to see one, let alone the early middle-aged man in badly crumpled blue suit who followed the policeman. Besides, he had not yet had time to appoint the Royal Physician. What were the Usurpers up to now? And how was he to know that this man – this undistinguished-looking man – was a doctor at all rather than, say, a poisoner? Perhaps the situation was coming to a head.

'Mr Smith?' said the alleged doctor after the policeman had left. 'Mr Reginald Smith?'

He had had to glance down at a piece of paper on a clipboard that he held to check that he had got it right.

'We're His Majesty King Reginald, the First of that Name,' said the King, suddenly having tired of this charade.

'Ah,' said the doctor.

'Yes,' said the King, 'and we're getting a little tired of this pretence that no one knows who we really are.'

'Was it you who wrote the letters to... to...?'

'Mrs Elizabeth Windsor? Yes, it was we,' he said, minding his grammar. 'And if we may say so, we have shown remarkable patience and restraint. So far,' he added ominously.

'So you are the King?" said the doctor (if that is what he was), whose tone was neutral, neither rude nor deferential. In the context, however, any tone other than deferential was insolent.

'Of course.'

'Since when?'

Since when? What an absurd question! 'Since the death of our mother, Her Majesty Queen Doris, of course.'

'When was that?'

'Ten years ago.'

'And when did you first realise that you were king?'

His Majesty thought for a moment.

'About four weeks ago.' He described the passage of the Rolls-Royce past his window as he was looking out.

'Could it have meant something else?' asked the doctor, or Usurpers' spy.

'What else could it have meant?' His Majesty looked puzzled by the question.

The doctor (or whoever he was) wrote things down on the paper on his clipboard. After a couple of minutes he said, 'I would like you to come into hospital for a while, for a rest.'

The King was taken aback.

'Why? Whatever for?'

'You've been overdoing it lately, not sleeping, not taking care of yourself and so forth.'

'And if I don't agree?' The King had detected a hint of menace or threat in the supposed doctor's manner.

'Well,' said the latter, as if deliberating as he went along, 'then I would have to ask one of my colleagues to come and see you.'

'And then?'

'And then… well, if he agreed with me, you'd have to come into hospital anyway.'

'So either I agree or you force me?'

The doctor – clearly now the Usurper's pawn – made no answer. The Usurper was using Soviet tactics, but in the end they would do her no good, the truth would out. He might as well go along with the charade for the time being: another few days would make no difference. In fact, it would only add to his subjects' outrage when they learnt the truth.

'All right, I agree,' said the King. The Usurper's pawn let out a sigh of relief, or like a balloon releasing some of its air. 'On one condition,' the King added.

'What's that?' asked the pawn nervously.

'That I am addressed by my proper title.'

'I can guarantee that,' said the supposed doctor. 'We address everyone correctly, I hope.'

On this understanding, the King agreed to go to hospital, that is to say the C. G. Jung Ward of the Nelson Mandela Mental Health and Wellbeing Centre in Much Frampton, the town next to Forehampton on the main road to the north.

He was taken there by the police, who assiduously, almost pedantically, returned to him the contents of his pockets when he arrived at the police station. They were removed from him again when he arrived at the Mental Health and Wellbeing Centre.

His subjects in C. G. Jung Ward were a strange and unattractive group. There were the nurses, so-called, who sat much of the day in a kind of glass cage with a locked door, in which they chatted and drank coffee, but rushed out whenever there was a commotion outside. They were mainly very fat, especially the women among them. What went on inside the glass cage was like a silent film to those outside it, who assumed that the nurses were hatching a plot against them.

Those who were called clients were mostly young, who either lay on their beds smoking illicitly or loped round the day-room like caged animals, though with earphones through which excitatory music was relayed. A large screen, constantly illuminated, broadcast chat shows to which no one paid any attention. The clients wore tracksuits and half of them baseball caps, as if expecting rain or blinding sunlight. To speak to them – not that there was a reason to do so – you had to make yourself heard through their music and self-absorption. Their main reason to talk to one another was to obtain cannabis or other drugs, smuggled in by their visitors by a variety of means.

No one would be able to say after his sojourn that the King did not know his people or that he had been cut off from reality by court etiquette. But such knowledge was nevertheless painful and unpleasant to acquire. No one in his right mind would wish to stay here a moment longer than necessary.

The nurses spoke to His Majesty with a combination of amusement and pity. Having revealed who he thought he was, he did not think it worthwhile again to try to conceal it from the nurses. Some of them, in their more jocular moments, referred to him as 'His Majesty,' which never failed to produce a giggle among them.

After a few days, some of the most unpleasant that he had ever spent, the King decided to play their game, if that was what they wanted. He would pretend not to be King and instead to be Reginald Smith: he guessed that he would be released from captivity quicker if he did. He would also take their silly tablets by which they seemed to set such store. They said that they would inject him if he didn't.

The nurses told the Usurper's pawn that he was a model patient. It was not, unfortunately, that the pills had no effect upon him: whereas his mind had been crystal clear, never clearer in fact, it began to grow clouded and sluggish, as if a fog had en-

tered his skull. He experienced a strange combination of leth-
argy and agitation, the former interior and the latter exterior
to his mind; and although he was still King, it seemed not to
matter as much as it had. Now, whenever he was asked who he
was, he replied, like a soldier being asked his number, 'Reginald
Smith.'

After two weeks, a nurse in woollen leggings and a long
dress too tight for her that revealed the contours of her obesity
informed him that he was now better and would be fit to return
home, where he would receive regular visits from the 'team.'
But, she added sternly, he would have to continue to take his
pills if he did not want to return to hospital.

His Majesty returned to 23, Magnolia Drive. There was a
letter awaiting him from the Director of Human Resources of
the county's Department of Leisure, Culture, Sport and Diver-
sity:

Dear Mr Smith,

Following the closure of Forehampton Branch Library,
an exciting new opportunity has arisen at Minchampton
Library and Resource Centre for part time work, four
mornings a week from 9.30 am to 12.30 pm.

Your role would be as a Reading Facilitator. I enclose
an application form if you are interested. Applications
must be received by 15th May.

The county is an equal opportunity employer and all
posts are subject to medical examination.

Yours sincerely,

May 15th was long past. Minchampton was more than an
hour away by bus or car. His Majesty ignored the letter as being
beneath his notice. He resolved to write to Mrs Elizabeth Windsor instead – after he had had a rest.

- 9 -
Facing the Music

John Ruskin House, a concrete block of twenty-four floors, had a hundred and twenty-four flats, so it was only to be expected that a wide variety of people lived in it. There was, for example, Flying Pete, who had a flat on the seventeenth floor and who had installed a special window from which he abseiled his way down the facade of the building, not trusting to the lifts (he said). And there was Fireman Charlie, who started rather than extinguished fires. When he ran out of money in the winter because of his drug bills, and his electricity was cut off for non-payment, he would warm himself around the fire he made from his furniture, which was soon replaced by the Social. There was no point in evicting him because he would only have to have been housed somewhere else; and the fires were never very serious. The fire brigade extinguished them in minutes.

Fred Roberts was an unusual, almost eccentric, tenant of John Ruskin House: he gave no trouble and paid his rent. This was despite being only a postman, poorly paid and with little money to spare for his amusements. He was a very quiet, solitary man, shy to the point of timidity, aged about forty. He kept himself to himself, blushed if a woman spoke to him, and his pleasure was birdwatching. Needless to say, the vicinity of John Ruskin House was not a haunt of birds, bar the odd sparrow and an occasional crow feeding on the carcass of a cat squashed in the road by a young driver in a stolen car careering away from a drug deal. So Fred would take himself off at weekends by cycle to a semi-rural area over ten miles away where he would watch a greater variety of birds, keeping a meticulous record of those that he saw.

Fred had to leave early for work, usually about five in the morning. It was only about that time that John Ruskin House fell silent: until then it was a hive of activity of various kinds. The walls between the flats were thin, presenting hardly any obstruction to the passage of sound, and the tenants, mostly, were not averse to noise, rather the reverse: it was silence that made them uncomfortable. Everything could be heard through the walls: from the sounds of eating to lovemaking and arguments, from the flats one or two doors away and from the floors above and below. Parties sometimes shook the whole building, as in an earth tremor; it was difficult to distinguish between the sound of people enjoying themselves and of someone being murdered. The one, indeed, had sometimes followed the other; most of the violence was the result of the imbibition of drugs or over the possession of a girlfriend.

But it was music that disturbed Fred the most. It throbbed though John Ruskin House like a disordered heartbeat, or disordered heartbeats, several strains at a time, usually with lyrics proclaiming a hatred of women and the world. Fred disliked it, and one could not even say that he was used to it. Rather he was like a man born in a very hot climate who made what arrangements he could to avoid the worst of the heat. He had experimented with various kinds of earplugs and found the most efficient, or least deficient, of them; he had suspended rugs on his walls to absorb some of the sound, but in summer they lent an unpleasant dusty stuffiness to his low-ceilinged flat. Being on the fifteenth floor, it was only natural that his windows, as a precaution, should open only half an inch and hardly let any air in or out.

A new tenant moved in below, when the old was sentenced to life imprisonment for a gang kidnap and murder in another part of the city. The flat had lain empty for eleven months despite the housing crisis; then Ezekiel, known as Zek, moved in.

Zek, who was probably about forty, had the longest dreadlocks anyone had ever seen. One's first thought on seeing them was like that of many people on seeing the rooms in Versailles: how were they kept clean? Perhaps they weren't. Zek's eyes were always red-rimmed from smoking ganja, which he regarded, or said he regarded, as a religious duty; he was tall and gangling and loose-limbed. If asked about his work, he said that he was a DJ, though really he was, if not a man about town exactly, at least a man about slum. Like many of the residents of John Ruskin House, he lived between the economic cracks. His proudest boast was that he had fathered seventeen children, though no one, perhaps not even he, knew whether this was true.

One thing was certain: he so loved his music – reggae and rap – that he considered that everyone else should hear, if not listen to, it. Unfortunately, he was more or less nocturnal, becoming active at seven or eight in the evening. He went to bed at eight or nine in the morning, unless he had a tryst somewhere else in the city.

He spent several nights a week at home, however, and on those nights he played his music as if he were trying to fill a large vessel with it. The sound went through the walls and ceilings like radiation. It was proof against ear-plugs, which it made tingle in the ears, and it throbbed on for hours, like a migraine headache. It made all the previous noise in Johns Ruskin House seem like silence.

The first time it started, it had an effect on Fred like an electric shock: it gave him a jerk. He thought at first it could not last, not at that volume, that no one could possibly tolerate, let alone want, music at such a volume for long, for more than a few minutes. But on the contrary, it went on and on. In fact, it lasted the whole night.

Well, Fred told himself, it was his neighbour's first night in his new flat: perhaps it was really something to celebrate in his life. Maybe he had been homeless before and finally finding a roof over his head was a great relief to him. You had to make allowances.

The following morning, Fred, who loved his work and prided himself on doing it well, was exhausted. He had no more than dozed during the night, waking at short and regular intervals, woken by an exceptionally loud bass thump, or an enraged line angrily intoned rather than sung:

'I got a case of spittin' in a motherfucker's face...'

At least not having slept the previous night would mean that Fred would sleep well the following night.

But it was not to be. At eight o'clock the following evening, the bass began to thump again and Fred's flat to vibrate to it. The angry lyrics filled the air once more: they came through both foam and wax ear-plugs. But Zek's exuberance would surely die down sooner rather than later; besides, you didn't go to your neighbour to complain only two days after he had moved in, because he might be your neighbour for years. In a place like John Ruskin House you had to get on, even with those whose habits you did not like.

Two nights without proper sleep, though, gave Fred a leaden feeling in his skull and limbs. It was not a headache that he had exactly, but a sensation of not quite being in the world, as if the world were merely projected on a screen around him, of everything passing him by while he struggled to keep his eyes open. His eyelids felt like heavy metal shutters.

The third night was similar and the following day he was aware that he was making mistakes in his delivery round. The fourth night he decided to say something to Zek.

He went down the fire-escape-cum-stairwell to the floor below, to Zek's flat. Where there had once been an electric bell on the door jamb, there was now only a hole with a wire coming out, like a worm emerging from its tunnel. The flap of the aluminium letter-box was too thin and flimsy to make much of a sound, certainly none that could be heard over the music. There was nothing for it but to knock on the door itself, hard enough to be heard but not so hard as to destroy the thin plywood panel (front doors in John Ruskin House were either of plywood or reinforced steel installed at the tenant's expense). Fred made a fist and banged on the door like a hammer delicately employed.

There was no reply. Occasionally the sound of raucous female laugher made itself heard above the music. Fred tried again, with the same result. He gave up and returned to his own flat.

The music continued almost every night. Fred decided that he would have to tackle Zek during the day, when he was sleeping rather than playing his music. He could have no excuse then for not answering the door. One afternoon, Fred went to Zek's door and knocked.

At first there was no reply. Fred knocked again and then a third time. He heard the sound of padding feet slowly approaching the door, which then opened tentatively to reveal a bleary Zek in some kind of draped garment of many colours of vaguely African inspiration (though made in China). Zek was half-asleep, half-intoxicated.

'What you want, man?' he asked.

'I want to ask you to turn your music down,' said Fred. 'It's stopping me from sleeping.'

'I'm not playing no music,' said Zek.

'Not now,' said Fred. 'At night. It keeps me awake and I have to go to work in the morning.'

Zek was silent for a moment, as if he had to resolve unfamiliar concepts in his mind.

'I gotta right to play my music.'

'Couldn't you play it less loud?' asked Fred. 'It comes through the floor and makes everything shake.'

Zek looked at Fred. He was dealing with a madman, someone of no sense.

'It's only music, man. Everyone likes music.'

'But...'

Fred had no more time to explain or discuss. Zek closed the door, muttering something about not being left in peace to sleep.

Fred's only recourse now was to appeal to the authorities. Appealing to the authorities was not popular with the residents of John Ruskin House, who thought of them as the enemy; appealing to them about other residents was just one step below informing to the police. To be a snitch or a grass was fraught with the danger of retaliation. But by now Fred was so deprived of sleep that he could hardly hold himself upright without swaying. All his thoughts, all his desires, were about sleep. Sleep for him was now the highest imaginable good.

On one of his days off, he went to the council's Housing Office. He took a ticket from the dispenser which informed him that he was sixty-seventh in line. There were only three staff answering enquiries (separated from the enquirers by thick shatter-proof glass that necessitated speaking through a microphone that the staff could turn off at will), but Fred decided to wait however long it took. Finally, his turn was called.

He explained why he had come to a fat lady behind the glass who seemed to overflow her seat. Before he had finished, she told him that he had come to the wrong place: he needed the E.P.U., the Environmental Protection Unit, which was on the other side of the city.

Again, there was nothing for it but to go: but now it was too late in the day, he would have to wait for another of his days off.

He was unlucky in the day he chose: the Environmental Protection Unit was away at a team-building meeting at the Hampton Health Spa and Conference Hotel, where they were devising a mission statement (they decided on 'Building a Greener City'). The Unit would re-open as usual on the following Monday, but Fred didn't have a day off until a week after that.

The woman to whom Fred spoke at the E.P.U. was an African whose accent Fred, no cosmopolitan despite living in John Ruskin House, found difficulty in understanding. However, he gathered that she would ask the N.N.T. (the Noise Nuisance Team) to investigate his complaint, with the proviso that being very busy, it might not make it to John Ruskin House for several weeks. It would record the noise levels in his flat over a period of twenty-four hours.

Luckily Fred was in when the N.N.T. arrived in the form of a man in blue overalls and a tin box of instruments. Unluckily, however, Zek was away when he arrived. His brother had been shot dead in Jamaica, and Zek had decided to combine the funeral with a holiday.

'It's no use doing it now,' said Fred, as the man searched suitable places to install his monitors. 'My neighbour who makes the noise is away.'

'Look, mate,' said the man in overalls, 'it's no use telling me. I'm only the technician. I don't give the orders, I do what them up there tell me to do.'

He came again at about the same time the following day and removed the monitors. Fred had been sleeping better than he had since Zec first took the tenancy. Two weeks later – Zek was back now and a full night's sleep was again impossible – Fred received a letter.

Dear Mr Roberts [it said],

Our investigations are now complete and have established that the noise levels in your flat in John Ruskin House are well within the limits laid down by Health and Safety Regulations.

Yours sincerely.
Noise Nuisance Team
Working for a Greener City

'You should've been here last night!' shouted Fred in his empty flat when he had read the letter. Not normally a violent man, he crumpled the letter into a ball and threw it across the room, which he regretted at once having done.

What to do now? He would have to return to the Environment Protection Unit to explain that their decision was erroneous and based on a false assessment, without knowledge of the real situation. He would ask them to repeat their tests. He fetched the letter from where it had landed and straightened it out. He might need to show it at the Unit.

The African lady was not there when he returned: instead an Albanian, or something like that. Fred explained to her why he had come.

'This letter says there was no heavy noise,' she said, looking over the letter that Fred had proffered.

'Yes, but my neighbour wasn't there when they measured it.' She looked bored by what he said.

'What you want we should do about it?' she asked.

'Well, Zek's back, so you could measure it again.'

'Who's Zek?'

'My neighbour. He's there now. He makes all the noise. If you measured it tonight, you'd realise.'

'You want we measure it second time?'

'Yes.'

She looked shocked, almost disgusted.

'Not possible,' she said. 'Unit's very busy. Every day new complaints. We can't manage all. Waiting list of more than three months. We can't go back to same place twice. This would be unfair.'

'But Zek wasn't there the first time.'

'Rules mean one time only measurement. Policy because fair. We can't be favourite of some people because they say they want second, third, fourth measurement, otherwise waiting list two years. You are no special.'

'But it'll be terrible tonight.'

'You think you special, exceptional?' she asked. 'Look.' She held up a document that as several pages long. 'List of people waiting. Not possible to do two times, only one time. The rules are rules.' So saying, she put down the document as if slamming a door.

Fred realised he could get no further and there was no point in staying. But he really couldn't see that he was being unreasonable: Zek's music was abominably loud.

He had to think of something else. He decided that he would bang on Zek's door every afternoon after he had played his music the night before: a faint taste of his own medicine.

He put this idea into practice. The first time, Zek opened the door and peered out at Fred.

'Last night, you played your music very loud and I couldn't

sleep,' said Fred.

'I gotta right if I feel like it,' said Zek, and shut the door.

Fred went the next day and said the same thing.

'Look, I told you, I gotta right, so fuck off.' Zek slammed the door.

But Fred didn't give up: he went a third time.

'I'm telling you one last time,' said Zek angrily.

Fred had nothing to lose. He was desperate and took no notice of Zek's air of menace. He went a fourth time, but Zek did not answer. He was lying low; Fred returned upstairs to his own flat.

Later that afternoon, while it was still light, Fred heard a knock at his front door.

'Who is it?' he called.

'Police. Open up.'

Fred opened his door. Before him stood two policemen dressed as if for guerrilla war. They worse bullet- and stab-proof vests that inflated their size like balloons, and from their belts dangled truncheons, a couple of canisters and a pair of handcuffs. Their radios crackled and each had a microphone attached to the earpiece in one of their ears.

'Are you Fred Roberts?' one of them asked.

'Yes, that's me.'

'We've had a complaint of racial harassment against you,' said the other policeman.

Fred looked bemused and said nothing.

'Your neighbour downstairs says you've been harassing him.'

'It's the other way round,' said Fred. 'He plays his music very loud all the time.'

'We can't hear nothing,' said one of the policemen, cocking his ear.

'At night, he plays it at night,' said Fred. 'He sleeps during the day.'

'He's just called us, so he's not asleep.'

'That's 'cause I just went round and complained.'

'So you *are* harassing him?'

'I'm asking him to turn his music down.'

'Every day?'

'For the last four days. The council won't do nothing, they say there's no noise coming from his flat.'

'We're arresting you on suspicion of racially-aggravated harassment,' said one of the policemen.

Fred, the mildest of men, saw red and lost his temper.

'Fuck off, the pair of you!' he shouted, and slammed his door.

The policemen did not go away. They banged on Fred's door and shouted 'Open up, open up!' But Fred did not open his door.

The policemen had no choice but to force an entry. Luckily, the door was one of the flimsy ones. Having kicked it a few times, they had to put their shoulders to it only once for it to give way. They burst in and found Fred, not a very formidable proposition, standing in his living room.

'We're arresting you as well on a charge of resisting arrest,' one of the policemen said.

They handcuffed Fred and led, or pulled, him out of John Ruskin House. He spent the night in the cells at the police station and they put him before the magistrate in the morning. The police objected to bail on two grounds: the first that he would return to harassing his neighbour, considering how he had already done it several times; and second because his conduct had demonstrated that he might not answer to bail when the time came to do so. His lawyer, the duty solicitor, a man with flat feet and beery breath, said nothing. The magistrate agreed with the police and remanded Fred into Greenfields Prison.

Fred was processed there in the usual way. He was given some ill-fitting clothes, asked some perfunctory medical questions, and given a little bag containing some tobacco and biscuits. This was removed from him by a prisoner much larger than he, who took it as a matter of course.

Fred was directed to a cell next to that of a man with long dreadlocks who hardly grunted at him as Fred arrived. He had in his possession a large silvery contraption for playing music, and all evening he played a few discs over and over again, very loudly.

'I got a case of spittin' in a motherfucker's face...'

When they opened Fred's cell in the morning, they found him hanging from a rope which he had made of his bedclothes.

The report of the official enquiry afterwards concluded:

In summary, we could find no evidence of any act or omission that could have prevented Mr Roberts' suicide.

- 10 -
A Life

'It's ruined my life, doctor,' said the woman. 'I've never been the same since.'

The doctor, a middle-aged man in a tweed jacket and woollen tie, wrote down her words. Then he looked up at her.

'Tell me what happened,' he said. 'What ruined your life?'

'Taking them pills,' she said.

She had been encouraged to come by a lawyer who had advertised for victims of medical accident and injury. She had gone to see him in his office and he had told her that she had a good case, that compensation was due, but that first she would have to be examined by a doctor who would ask her a lot of questions. There was nothing to worry about, though, it was a pure formality. Then he mentioned a larger sum of money than she had ever imagined possible, even existent.

'Will there be a court case?' she asked. The thought of being in the witness box made her blood run cold and her knees go weak, even though she was sitting.

'Oh no,' said the lawyer. 'It never comes to that. They will settle. They always do.'

So now she was sitting beside the doctor's desk, with one of her elbows resting on it. She was in her middle thirties but determined to look younger. Cigarettes had kept her thin.

'I took the pills what the doctor gave me,' she said, 'and I immediately began to feel funny.'

'Your doctor, your general practitioner?'

'Yes, Dr Patel. He's retired and now you have to see anyone who's available.'

'I see. And why did you go to Dr Patel?'

'I wasn't feeling well.'

If she had been observing closely, she would have seen a faint elevation of the doctor's eyebrow.

'Do you remember if Dr Patel diagnosed anything?'

'A touch of blood pressure, I think he said it was.'

The doctor wrote this down too. High blood pressure is a symptomless disease until disaster happens or it is treated, and so Dr Patel must have used an incidental finding to explain what he otherwise could not explain. Patients always preferred a bogus explanation to no explanation at all.

'These pills, do you remember what they were?'

'Little yellow ones.'

'How many did your take?'

'Dr Patel said to take two, one in the morning and one in the evening, and an extra one if I felt bad.'

'And did you ever take an extra one?'

'All the time,' the woman said. 'I felt bad all the time. They made me feel awful.'

'Why did you take them, then?'

'Dr Patel said I should.'

'And in what way did they make you feel awful?'

'In every way. I was dizzy, I was tired all the time, I couldn't do nothing, I had panic attacks, I just wanted to lie down all the while. I cried all the time.'

'How long have you been taking the pills?'

The woman thought as deeply as she was able.

'A long time,' she said.

'How long?' asked the doctor. 'Roughly, it doesn't matter exactly.'

'I think it must be fifteen years. Just after my first termination, it must have been.'

'We'll come to that in a minute,' said the doctor. 'But first let me be clear: I don't want to make a mistake. You've been taking the pills for fifteen years?'

'Yes, about.'

'And they make you feel terrible?'

'Yes.'

'Did you ever try stopping them?'

'No. I mean, yes.'

'No, yes. Which is it?'

'Well, I did try once.'

'And what happened?'

'I felt awful, worse.'

'In what way?'

'In every way. I felt dizzy, tired all the time, I had panic attacks, I couldn't do nothing. I had to lie down all the while and I cried.'

'That was what you were like anyway.'

'It was much worse.'

'And when were you last quite well?'

The woman searched her mind like someone looking for something that isn't there.

'Before I started taking them pills,' she said.

'But you started taking them because you weren't feeling well.'

'Yes, but not like this, doctor.'

The doctor passed his hands over his eyes as if wiping something away.

'I'm going to ask you a lot of questions about yourself,' he said.

'The lawyer said you was going to.'

'Did he tell you anything else?'

'He said them pills ruined my life and I would get compensation.'

'Yes, well... where were you born?'

The woman named an unpropitious place to start one's life.

'Are your parents still alive?'

'My mother is.'

'And your father?'

'I never knew him. He left when I was little. He used to knock her about, my mother said. He had other women too. And he drank.'

'So your mother brought you up alone?'

'Sometimes.'

'Sometimes?' The doctor sounded surprised.

'I was sent to my nan's sometimes, when Mum couldn't cope, like.'

'Cope? With what?'

'Well, you see, sometimes she had… sometimes I had…'

What was the word for it, exactly? A rose is sometimes not as sweet by any other name.

'A stepfather?' suggested the doctor. 'Your mother had a boyfriend?'

'Yes, only they never stayed for very long. She had to kick them out.'

'Always the same one?'

'No, there was different ones.'

'What were they like?'

'Most of them was horrible. Bill was all right, he went to work, like, and he didn't drink, but Mum said he was boring so she kicked him out too.'

'Do you have any brothers and sisters?'

To the doctor's surprise, this question – so ordinary, so banal, so routine – produced something convulsive in the woman. When the wave had passed through her, she said:

'One brother and two half-sisters.'

There followed a silence.

'Do you still see them?' asked the doctor.

'I don't have nothing to do with them.'

'Why not?'

'He interfered with us, like.'

'With all of you?'

'Yes, only when I told Mum, the others denied it and my mum called me a lying slut. She said that if I ever said it again, she's throw me out.'

'How old were you?'

'Fifteen. I left home when I was sixteen.'

'Where did you go?'

'I went to live with Harry.'

'Who was he?'

'A man what I knew.'

'How old was he?'

'Harry? He was about forty.'

'How did you know him?'

'I met him down the park. He used to give me cigarettes.'

'What did he do?'

'What do you mean?'

'For a living.'

'Harry? He didn't do nothing. He was on the Sick, so he couldn't work.'

'What illness did he have?'

'Harry? He took drugs. He smoked dope all the time.'

'What was he like?'

'He was all right some of the time. But sometimes he smacked me about a bit. His eyes would go, and then he'd grab me by the throat.'

'How long did you stay with him?'

'With Harry? About a year, maybe two.'

'Then what happened?'

'I caught pregnant for him. He wanted me to get rid of it, but I didn't want to, so I left him.'

'Where did you go?'

'Me? The council gave me a flat.'

'You had the baby?'

'Yes, she's eighteen now and got two kids of her own.'

'So you're a grandmother?'

'Yes.'

'Do you see your grandchildren?'

'No.'

'Why not?'

'She's with this crack dealer feller. He's in and out of prison. He don't like me.'

'The children are his?'

'One of them.'

'Do you have other children?' asked the doctor.

'I got two. They're still at home with me. They're still at school.'

The doctor paused.

'Doing well?' he asked.

'Dwayne, he's naughty. He won't sit still, he runs about all the time. He won't do what he's told. He steals. Sometimes he wears me out.'

'And the other?'

'Kayley? She's a little madam.'

'And their father?'

The woman gave a little snort of derision: a stupid question.

'They're no use.'

'They don't come to see them?'

'I haven't seen Dwayne – he's Dwayne's Dad – since I caught pregnant for him. He's off the scene completely. He was never no good.'

'And Kayley's father?'

'Courtney? Courtney's a... a...'

She searched for a word but couldn't find it.

'A nuisance?' suggested the doctor.

'You can say that again,' said the woman, as if shocked by the doctor's feeble description of Courtney. Was he trying to make excuses for him? 'I've had to have the police out to him,' she said. 'Not that it makes no difference. It doesn't stop him.'

'Stop him from what?'

'From coming round and banging on the door.'

'You let him in?'

'I have to.'

'Why?'

'He'd put my windows through if I didn't.'

'I see,' said the doctor. 'What's he like, Courtney?'

'He's very jealous. He calls me a slag, things like that. He won't leave me alone.'

'How long were you with him?'

'We never lived together, nor nothing like that. He always

had his own place. He said he needed his space. He would just come and go as he pleased.'

'Was he always jealous?'

'Not to begin with, not for the first few weeks. He treated me like a queen. He even bought me flowers.'

'And then what?'

'He hit me.'

'Why?'

'I had too much makeup on, he said. What did I need it for? He said it was because I was seeing someone else, or trying to.'

'But you weren't?'

'No, of course not. I'm not like that.'

'What happened next?'

'He said if I told him who it was, he'd forget it and we could start again.'

'But of course you couldn't tell him because there wasn't anyone.'

'Yes. So he smacked me again. He broke my jaw.'

'You had to go to hospital?'

'Yes, but I told them it was the front door slammed in my face from the wind.'

'They believed you?'

'I don't know. I was afraid of him and what they would do to him if I told the truth.'

'And the children?'

'They went to his mother's until I come out of the hospital.'

'And you took Courtney back?'

'He said he was sorry, like, so what could I do? He said he couldn't help it and it would never happen again. And he was Kayley's dad.'

'But she wasn't born yet, was she?' asked the doctor.

'No, but I was pregnant for her.'

'And you wanted her?'

'No, I wanted them to take her away with an operation but Courtney wouldn't hear of it. He said a baby would make things better between us.'

'And you believed him?'

'I did at first. I thought a baby would make him grow up because he was just a boy, really.'

'But it didn't?'

'I only discovered later that he had baby-mothers all over the place. That's why, when I caught pregnant for him again, I had it took away. He was furious and started hitting me again, because he said it was another man's baby.'

'And what happened after?'

'I tried everything. I've had the police out on him, I even went to court for him. They said he couldn't come anywhere near me, but he didn't take no notice. I called the Social too.'

'What did they do?'

'They put in a panic button connected straight to the police station what I can press if he breaks in, like.'

'And have you ever pressed it?'

'Yes, a few times.'

'And what happens then?'

'The police come and take him away, like.'

'And then?'

'And then he comes back the next day, so I don't press it no more.'

'Because there's no point.'

'No, because he got one of his mates to speak to me in the street.'

'What did he say?'

'He said if I pressed that button again, he's break my fucking legs.'

The doctor put his pen down for a moment. Then he picked it up again.

'Let's move on to something else,' he said. 'Have you ever worked?'

'No,' said the woman. 'I wanted to be a nurse, but then I met Harry and then Dwayne.'

'And you haven't worked since? Not ever?'

'No, I haven't been able to.'

'And you don't work now?'

'I can't.'

'Why not?'

'I'm on the sick, aren't I?'

'What with?'

'Depression. I take them pills for it. They make me feel awaful.'

'So you can't work?'

'No, I feel too bad. Them pills have ruined my life, I've never been the same since I started taking them.'

The doctor put his pen down again and passed his hand once more over his face. When it had cleared it, so to speak, he said:

'Thank you. I think that's all I need. Do you have any questions?'

The woman thought for a moment.

'Yes,' she said. 'Will there be any compensation?'

The doctor pulled in his lips as if to derive some nourishment from them. Then he said:

'It's not for me to say. You'll have to ask your lawyer.'

'Thank you, doctor,' said the woman. She left and closed the door behind her.

The doctor wrote his report to the lawyer shortly afterwards and enclosed his bill with it. Oh yes, there would be compensation all right.